Again Rona woke 　　　　　　　　　　l
all around her. It filled the room, calling ner, and
again it seemed to be coming up through the
floor.

Wide awake now, she slipped out of bed and
into her dressing gown. Flying on silent feet
she raced down the passage, determined to
trace the source of the eerie sound before it faded.
She let herself out the back door and ran along
the side of the house to the storage cellar under
her bedroom. She lifted the latch and pushed
open the heavy door. It was cold inside. The
darkness wrapped itself around her like a musty
blanket as the door swung shut behind her.

Dong — dong — dong — dong . . . The sound
was closer than ever. It had to be coming up from
under the ground, but how?

THE
SHEARWATER
BELL

MARGARET BEAMES

SCHOLASTIC

AUCKLAND SYDNEY NEW YORK TORONTO LONDON

First published Scholastic New Zealand Limited, 1997
Private Bag 94407, Greenmount, Auckland 1730, New Zealand.

Scholastic Australia Pty Limited
PO Box 579, Gosford, NSW 2250, Australia.

Scholastic Inc
555 Broadway, New York, NY 10012-3999, USA.

Scholastic Canada Ltd
123 Newkirk Road, Richmond Hill, Ontario L4C 3G5, Canada.

Scholastic Limited
1-19 New Oxford Street, London, WC1A 1NU, England.

© Margaret Beames, 1997
ISBN 1-86943-354-8

9 8 7 6 5 4 3   8 9 / 9   0 1 2 3 4 / 0

Edited by Penny Scown
Cover illustration and design by Christine Dale
Typeset in 12/16pt New Baskerville
Printed in Malaysia

For Oliver
who shares a birthday
with this book

ONE

Twenty kilometres of dusty, bone-shaking, unsealed road after driving for hours and hours was almost too much to bear. Why would anyone want to live way out here, anyway? thought Rona. What would there be to do?

"Why?" she asked her mother.

"Why what?" Mum was concentrating on the road.

"Grandma — why doesn't she live in a town?"

"Call her Nan. She prefers Nan," said Mum.

"She grew up here. So did I."

Rona sighed. "But she doesn't have to stay here, miles from everywhere. So why does she?"

"When I come back for you, perhaps you'll be able to tell me," Mum said.

"I don't even know her," grumbled Rona.

Mum patted her knee. "It'll be all right, you know," she promised. "Her bark's worse than her bite."

What is she, thought Rona, a Doberman? She was still a little stunned at the way her life had been changed so dramatically by a single telephone call. She and Mum had been watching television when it came, and the sudden loud ringing had startled them.

Mum was a long time answering the call and when she came back she was as white as a sheet, her dark eyes large with shock.

"There's been an accident," she said, sinking down onto the sofa as if all the strength had gone out of her. "A pile-up on the motorway into London."

"Dad! He's not — "

"No!" Mum answered quickly. "But he is in hospital, and it's serious. He's unconscious. I'll have to go over."

"And me!" Rona cried.

Mum shook her head. "No, lovey, you'll have to stay here. I wouldn't be able to look after you. I'll need to be at the hospital." She jumped up. "I must pack . . . and get on a flight. Oh, Lord, who do I call at this time of night?"

Somehow, after some frantic telephoning, a seat was booked on a flight to London. Mum's passport was found and her suitcase packed. There were more phone calls in the morning and at last Rona dared to ask, "What about me?"

"Oh, sweetie, you've been so good, not a word about yourself while I was rushing around panicking. You're going to Shearwater."

Shearwater! That was where Mum's mother lived. Rona had not been there since she was a baby. She could not remember in the least bit what it was like.

"Couldn't I stay with Joanne? Her mother wouldn't mind," she begged.

"I'm sure she wouldn't, but I don't know how long I'll be away," Mum explained. "I called the hospital again last night — it was daytime over there, of course, they're twelve hours behind us — but there's been no change. Dad's still deeply unconscious, and with a head injury like this . . . well, he could be in a coma for some time. Even if he comes round soon it'll be a while before he can travel all this way. I may be gone for weeks. I couldn't ask Judy to have you for so long."

And she doesn't really approve of Joanne's mother, thought Rona. She likes her because she's fun, but thinks she lets Joanne get away with too much.

"I thought you didn't like your mum," she said.

"Of course I do, she's my mother," Mum said, a bit desperately. "We — we just had a falling out."

Rona stared down at her feet, wishing she had more relations than just a grandmother who sounded pretty grim.

Mum tried to explain. "It's just that she was very strict with me when I was growing up — harder on me than she should have been, probably — so of course as soon as I was old enough to leave home, off I went.

"Then I met your father and we decided to get married. I took him to Shearwater to meet your Nan. She started telling me I was too young to get married and, well . . . you know Dad, he always says what he thinks. He told her it was. about time she stopped interfering and let me live my own life. They had an awful quarrel."

Mum fell silent. Rona wondered if Nan would be as hard on her. Then Mum gave a little laugh and added, "If she fusses over you, bosses you, don't worry about it. Just remember she means it for the best — though I couldn't see that when I was young."

"But I'll miss school." The summer term with softball and swimming had just begun. "Or will I have to go to school there, at Shearwater?"

Mum looked at her blankly. This was something she had not thought about. "There was a school there but I think it closed down. We'll have to see when you get there."

Rona sighed, but her mother said patiently, "I'm sorry, Rona, there just isn't anyone else."

Rona wasn't happy about going to stay with someone who was a stranger, even if she was her grandmother, and in a place where she might or might not go to school. It was not that she minded missing school — it was not knowing. She wanted to argue but knew that Mum had enough to worry about without that.

Immediately after breakfast, Mum loaded up the car with Rona's things and some food for the journey. Her own cases were left standing in the hall to be grabbed as soon as she returned, then she would hand the house keys to Joanne's mother next door and rush by taxi to the airport.

They set off and picked up Mum's airline ticket and traveller's cheques from the travel agent on their way through town before heading north.

It was mid-afternoon by the time they passed through the tiny fish-smelling village of Sandy Bay and saw the sea glittering on their left.

"Not a very original name," Mum remarked. "Last petrol, last shop, last everything until you drop off the edge of the world at Shearwater."

It was not quite the end, though, because there was a farm between the village and Nan's house. A sign on the gate offered: FRESH FISH, EGGS, VEGIES. Rona wondered if anyone ever passed the gate to buy them.

Mum stopped to let a herd of cows flow lazily around them on its way to be milked. A boy of about twelve followed behind, idly tapping the stragglers with a long stick. He waved as he passed them.

"You'll be able to fetch Nan's milk for her," said Mum. "I expect she still gets it from the farm. The Thompsons. They've lived there for yonks too." She peered in the rear-vision mirror at the boy, and exclaimed, "Good heavens! That must be Wiri. He was just a baby last time I saw him. He must be about your age."

"Are there any girls?" asked Rona, hopefully.

"There are three older children and I think there was another baby later, but Wiri was one on his own as far as age goes," Mum said vaguely. Rona sighed.

The road began to climb. The sea was still visible. "Varren's Bay," said Mum.

"Named after Nan?" asked Rona in surprise.

"Yes. Well, the family, anyway. Next along is Ship Cove, but you can't get down to that from the cliff."

They rattled over a cattle-stop set between gateposts and there ahead of them was Shearwater, sheltering in a hollow below a line of ancient black trees which lay almost on their sides where year after year the westerly winds had swept over them.

Mum cut the engine and it suddenly seemed very quiet. They got out of the car and headed towards the house. Rona listened: just the wind, the bleat of a lonely sheep, their feet crunching the gravel.

The house was long and low. The door stood open, but no one came out to meet them.

"Mother?" Mum called into the silence inside.

Behind the house was a vegetable patch, with rows of fresh green leafy things, neatly hoed. The rest of the garden, flowers and shrubs, rambled into the distance. Fat black hens scratched contentedly under fruit trees.

They returned to the car. Suddenly Mum nudged Rona and pointed. On the cliff beyond the house, gazing out over the sea, was a tall thin woman

11

with long white hair tied back like a girl's, the ends whipping around her shoulders in the wind — like a bird about to take to the air, thought Rona.

Mum leaned in through the car window and sounded the horn. Nan turned and saw them. She came away from the cliff top, striding back down to the garden through a little brown gate that was kept shut to keep the sheep out.

She and Mum just looked at each other for a moment, then Mum put her arms around Nan and hugged her. "It's been a long time," she said.

Nan nodded, standing as stiff as a board. "So this is Verona." Rona winced. No one called her that. "She's not much like you."

"No, she takes after her father," Mum said, carefully. "Anyway, thanks for letting her come to you."

"I've no quarrel with the child. And I'm sorry about Tom," Nan said, and some of the strain went out of Mum's face.

They sat down to a meal laid ready for them on the big scrubbed table in the kitchen. Rona wasn't hungry but she forced herself to eat so that Mum wouldn't worry. As the time came nearer for Mum to go, Rona tried to get used to the idea of being left there with her grandmother. She was a bit scared of her and so far had hardly raised her eyes higher than the bone carving Nan wore on a leather thong around her neck. It was a seabird of some kind, its slender wings spread wide in flight.

"You'll stay the night?" asked Nan.

"I can't," said Mum. "My plane goes at midnight. I have to go straight back and pick up my bags, then get over to the airport as fast as I can."

"Driving all that way in one day!" exclaimed Nan. "You should rest. I don't suppose you slept much last night."

"I'll sleep on the plane. Don't worry, I'll take care," Mum assured her.

Rona was suddenly scared. What if Mum fell asleep at the wheel? Or there was another accident? If anything happened to Mum she'd really be on her own. She wanted to shout at her not to go.

"Telephone from the airport before you take off," Nan said.

"It'll be so late. You'll be in bed," protested Mum.

"Call us," said Nan. It was an order and Mum nodded meekly.

It was time for her to go. She hugged Rona so tightly she could hardly breathe. "I'll give you a ring after I've seen your dad . . . and I'll write," she promised, "and you make sure you write back, you hear?"

Rona willed herself not to blink so that the tears brimming in her eyes wouldn't be squeezed out. She was almost glad when Nan gave Mum a little push towards the car. "Go on now — you'll miss that plane," Nan said.

They watched the car bump its way back down the road. Rona gave a sigh. Mum was gone. She felt very much alone. As Nan stared at the empty road, lost in thought, Rona looked at her properly for the first time.

She had a young face for a grandmother, but stern. Her eyes were like Mum's, very dark and bright, but they didn't smile very often.

Suddenly Nan seemed to remember that Rona was there.

"I've put you in your mother's room that she had when she was a little girl," she said, leading the way indoors and picking up Rona's suitcase. "Come on, and I'll show you where it is."

"That's my room," said Nan as they passed a door, half open, allowing a little light into the gloomy passage. "This is the bathroom. I'll explain about the hot water later."

Remembering Mum's stories about her childhood — an outside toilet and baths in a tin tub in the kitchen! — Rona was relieved to see that there was now a proper bathroom.

Right at the end of the long passage were two steps leading up to the room that was to be hers.

It was a pretty room, square with white painted walls. On one side the ceiling sloped down under the roof, and below it was a long bookcase filled with books that had been her mother's. A row of shabby dolls sat on an old settee. This room was a little higher than the rest of the house because underneath it was a cool storage cellar built into the sloping ground.

Nan went to the window and pushed it open to let in warm air that smelled of flowers and honey. Rona dumped her backpack and went to look, giving a little gasp as she saw the sea shining in the distance. Above it, the sun turned the clouds pink and blue. Later they would be stained violent orange and purple.

"You'll like this room," Nan told her.

Rona smiled. She loved it already. She bounced on the bed, which felt soft and springy. There was a twang from beneath and she glanced guiltily at her grandmother, but Nan did not appear to have noticed. "I'll leave you to unpack and settle in," she said. "Use the drawers and cupboards. You can do what you like in here. I expect you to keep it clean and tidy, but otherwise it's all yours." She left, closing the door behind her. Rona half expected to hear the lock click, keeping her in her place.

She looked in the empty wardrobe, picked up each of the old dolls on the settee and examined the books in the bookcase. Then she sat on the bed, thinking. Things were going to be very different here, that was for sure.

Late that night, Rona lay in bed, tired but sleepless. The bed was cosy and comfortable, but it wasn't the bed she was used to. And the silence! At home, even if the street was quiet you could always hear traffic droning in the distance, and sometimes the sirens of emergency vehicles rushing by. Aircraft flew over. Just through the wall Mum would have the television or the radio on.

Here there was nothing but the spooky moaning of the wind. It had grown rough and blustery during the long, silent evening and now it wailed around the house as if it wanted to get in.

It was dark, too. At home her room was lit by the glow of the street lamp outside, and whenever a car drove past she could watch the lights flicker across the ceiling from one side to the other.

Now the darkness pressed around her like black velvet. She opened her eyes wide, but she might as well have been blind for all she could see. The light switch was over by the door. What if she needed to get out in the night? She had left the door slightly ajar — but where was it? She began to panic.

Calm down, Rona, she told herself. It's only for

tonight. Ask Nan for a lamp or a torch tomorrow. Think about something else for now.

She thought about her father. He was often away. When Rona had been a baby, she and Mum had travelled with him on overseas assignments for his newspaper, but now she was older her parents did not want to disrupt her schooling, so she and Mum stayed home. She could not remember much about her early travels, but she knew she had been born in Verona, Italy, when Dad had been working in Europe for a year. Which reminded her . . .

I must tell Nan about my name, she thought. No one calls me Verona, not even Mum when she's mad at me. I'll —

She froze, as a distant, hollow donging quivered through the blackness around her. What on earth was that?

She waited, but the eerie sound was not repeated. Somewhere in the house a telephone began to ring.

Nan must have been sitting right beside it for it stopped almost immediately and soon a light came flickering along the passage. Now Rona knew where the door was, and when it opened she could see the room clearly by the light of her grandmother's torch.

Nan stood by the bed. "Are you awake, Verona?

That was your mother. She arrived at the airport safely. She'll be boarding now. She'll call again from London and let us know how your father is."

Rona released the breath she had been holding. "Thanks, Nan."

She wished Nan would sit on the bed for a few minutes, perhaps give her a hug like Mum always did when she said goodnight, but Nan did not seem to know about hugs. She stood there stiffly. "It's hot in here," she said. "Shall I open your window again?"

"Yes, please."

Now Rona could hear clearly a booming sound that she realised had been there all the time in the distance. "What's that? That booming."

"Only breakers crashing against the foot of the cliff," replied Nan. "The tide's high tonight. You'll get used to it, Verona."

"Nan?"

"Yes?"

"Could you please not call me Verona?"

"Is that not your name?"

"Well yes, it is, but I don't like it. Everyone calls me Rona."

And then she heard it again — that faraway, echoing clang.

"What *is* that?" she cried. "That clanging noise."

Nan was staring towards the window, although there was nothing to see but the flowered curtains that she had just redrawn.

"Nan?" Rona was sure she was listening, but Nan shook her head.

"It's nothing," she said firmly.

"It sounds like a bell."

"It's just some loose metal banging somewhere. Go to sleep."

"It's very dark," Rona murmured.

"Darkness never hurt anyone," said Nan. "Still . . . I suppose you're not used to it. Very well, you can have my torch. I'm not leaving a light burning all night."

Nan put the torch into Rona's hands. When she had gone, Rona switched it off then on again several times. She felt happier now that she had light at the press of a button, but she was left with a new thought to consider. Why had Nan lied about the bell?

TWO

Rona woke to the sound of someone chopping wood. It did not feel as if she had slept late, but without a watch or a clock in the room she could not be sure. She jumped out of bed and pulled aside the curtains.

It was a beautiful day and the wind had gone. A fat tabby and white cat, sunning itself on the stone path, looked up at her and opened its mouth in a silent miaow.

Rona made do with a quick wash, dressed quickly in yesterday's clothes and hurried along the passage to the kitchen. As she entered, Nan came in from the back yard carrying an armful of firewood.

"You're up then," she remarked. "What would you like for breakfast?"

"I usually have cereal," Rona ventured.

"How about a boiled egg and some toast?" Nan said as if Rona had not spoken. She put an egg in some water and told Rona to watch it. "When it starts to boil, give it three more minutes," she told her.

After the egg, which w~ ' ne just right, there was more toast w .n honey and a glass of milk. Nan had eaten breakfast earlier but she had another slice of toast and a cup of coffee while Rona ate hers.

"Now you know where everything is, you can make your own breakfast when you get up," Nan said. "I trust you're not one of those children who expect to have everything done for them?"

Rona shook her head.

The firewood was for a small woodburner. "It heats all our water," Nan explained. "You can have a shower in the evening and a wash in the morning, but don't waste water. It runs off the roof into a water tank, and although it hardly ever runs dry, we have to be careful."

There was a kettle on the burner, steaming softly. Nan poured some of the hot water into a bowl, topped the kettle up again and put it back to reheat.

"That's hot enough for washing up," she said. "I always keep a kettleful on the hob."

Rona saw that she was expected to wash her own dishes. At home she was used to a dishwasher. She was sure she could feel her grandmother watching her, seeing how awkward she was, but when she looked around, Nan was pulling on a pair of paint-splattered overalls.

"You'll have to amuse yourself today," she said. "You can go anywhere you like in the house or garden, but keep away from the cliff until I show you where it's safe to go. I haven't time today. I've been waiting for weeks for the wind to drop so I can get up on the roof."

Rona said she'd be fine on her own. In a way, it was a relief to be left to herself to get the feel of the place.

It did not take long to look around the house. There was the large sitting room, where they had sat the evening before, neither of them knowing what to say to the other. There were shelves and shelves of books, a radio and an old-fashioned record player, but no television.

Besides Nan's bedroom and her own, there was

another room with two single beds in it, and there was a large, messy room that appeared to be some kind of studio or workroom, full of painting easels and palettes, a lathe, tools for carving, grinding and polishing.

All through the house Rona had noticed arrangements of polished driftwood, and paintings on the walls. She realised now that Nan must have done these herself. She shut the door thoughtfully and went to explore the garden.

The sunlight was dazzling after the cool kitchen. The cat came to meet her, his fur hot from the sun as he rubbed against Rona's legs.

"That's Mungo," said a voice above her head, and Rona looked up, startled to see Nan perched on a ladder that was resting against the roof. "Mind out — I'm coming down."

Nan fetched a large can of green paint and a long-handled paint roller from a shed. Now Rona saw why her grandmother wanted to get on the roof.

"Here goes!" Nan announced. "Better keep clear unless you want green streaks in your hair!"

Rona stepped back hastily. She watched for a while as, with long sweeps of the roller, Nan began to turn the dull, faded brown of the roof to a fresh, shining green. It was clearly going to take her all day, so Rona set off to see what else there was to see. Mungo kept her company, not exactly walking with her, but stalking her from bush to bush wherever she went.

After circling the garden Rona was no nearer to solving the mystery of the bell she had heard during the night. The only place she had not looked was in a little brick shed with a locked door. There was nothing in the house or garden that could possibly have made that noise. She hadn't heard it again, but nor had she imagined it, and, what's more, Nan had heard it too.

The morning passed slowly. When Rona returned to the house Nan was still on the roof but there was an empty glass by the sink that had not been there before. Rona helped herself to a drink also. Then she fetched a book from her room and took it into the garden to read in the shade under the trees.

Along the road at the Thompsons' farm, four-year-old Sissie was making a trail. Just like Hansel and Gretel through the forest, she thought, except that her trail wasn't made of breadcrumbs and it wasn't through a forest. She was using her brother's marbles. The trail snaked across the yard and behind the woolshed.

Suddenly a quick brown hand snatched the bag

of marbles from her. "What are you doing with those?" Wiri demanded. "Where's the rest? There's only half of them here!"

"It's for my trail," Sissie cried. "You've got to follow the trail and pick the marbles up, like the birds picked up the crumbs."

"What are you talking about?" Wiri groaned. "I suppose it's another one of your stupid games."

"It was Hansel and Gretel," wailed Sissie, "and now you've ruined it!"

"Well you can use little stones like they did in the story the first time — and leave my things alone!"

Crossly, Wiri retraced Sissie's steps, gathering up the marbles. She was always messing about with his things. What he needed was a really safe hiding place that she wouldn't find.

Back in his room, he opened the cupboard built into the wall. If only it had a lock! The floorboard squeaked. It always did when he stood there. He tried to lift it, but it was nailed down solidly. The boards on the floor inside the cupboard did not look so firm, however. He grabbed his pocketknife and tried levering one up. To his delight it came up easily, revealing a space between the floor and the supporting struts below. It was dry and dusty — and Sissie would never find anything hidden there.

As he lay on his stomach staring down into the

dark space, his eyes focussed on what looked like a flat box. Had someone else used this hiding place before him? He reached in and pulled out a book, a shabby brown book bound in scuffed, water-stained leather. It looked pretty old. He sat on his bed, turning the book over in his hands. Then he opened its dusty covers.

From the first page to the last the book was filled with handwriting. The paper was yellow with age, the ink faded to a soft, dull brown. Wiri frowned as he tried to make out the words, but the lines were so close together and the spaces between the words so tiny that it was almost impossible. At the back he could see ragged edges where some pages had been torn out.

He turned to the front again. The writing straggled across the page in a thin, spidery scrawl. Every so often a thick line, when the ink ran too fast, almost blotted out a word. 'My name is —'

He was just beginning to decipher the next word when he heard Sissie calling him. Quickly he closed the book, tucking it inside his shirt. She wasn't getting her hands on this! He climbed over the windowsill, dropped onto the lean-to roof of the laundry and then down to the ground. There was one place where she couldn't get to him — the quince tree.

Lunchtime came. Nan cut some bread and they each made their own sandwiches at the kitchen table.

"I never bother much at midday," Nan said. "If you're hungry, just help yourself. There's always cheese and salad stuff and jam."

When Rona asked Nan about the little brick building, Nan said, "That's the generator in there. I run it for a few hours every day to top up the battery so we have light in the evening. I keep the shed locked because there's fuel in there." Now Rona understood why Nan had not wanted to leave the light on in the passage all night.

After lunch, Nan suggested that Rona fetch the milk from the Thompsons'. "It's not far," she said. "I usually cycle, but my bike would be too big for you, and your young legs won't find it any distance at all."

Rona was not so sure. It seemed a pretty long way to her. That was not her main worry though. "What if Mum phones while I'm away?"

"She won't phone today!" exclaimed Nan. "She'll still be travelling."

"Still?" echoed Rona. "All last night and all day today?"

"It's a long way to England," Nan said. "Twelve thousand miles and two refuelling stops. No, she'll telephone in the morning, you'll see."

Rona still wasn't keen to go to the farm by herself, but Nan was anxious to get back to painting the roof. She handed Rona two milk billies with wire handles. "Just follow the road, you can't get lost. You won't need any money — I pay at the end of the month."

I'd better go then, thought Rona reluctantly. At least it would be something to do.

Rona took her time, sauntering along, looking back now and then at the green roof with the figure in blue overalls clinging to it like a fly, getting smaller and smaller as she left it behind. Then the road curved and she was following the coast. The water looked cool and blue. She hoped Nan would find time to show her the way down to the beach soon.

She seemed to have been walking for hours before she came to the farm. A black and white collie was sleeping in the middle of the gateway. Rona looked at it warily. Dogs could be tricky. Perhaps she could creep past without waking it. She was still metres away from it, however, when it heard her and stood up, yawning and stretching and coming to meet her. It walked beside her up the track.

The farm appeared to be deserted. She tapped on the front door but no one came. The dog was watching her from the corner of the house, waiting.

It wagged its tail. As Rona went towards it, it trotted ahead of her to an open door at the side of the house and barked once.

A woman came out, wiping her floury hands on her apron. A small girl peeped out from behind her. "What is it, Pru?" the woman was saying. "A customer?" Then she saw Rona and smiled. "You must be Mrs Varren's granddaughter. She said you were coming on a visit."

"Yes. Nan sent me for the milk."

"Give me your billies," said Mrs Thompson, taking them from the girl's hands. "The cowshed's around here."

The dairy part of the cowshed was a long, low, cool room. It had white painted walls and a shining stainless steel chiller that the milk, still warm from the cows, ran through before going into a vat to be collected by the milk tanker. The concrete floor had been scrubbed and hosed down and water, milky-white with pine disinfectant, still lay in the cracks.

"So, how are you liking life in the country?" Mrs Thompson asked. "You'll be glad to get away from the city, I suppose."

"It's very quiet," said Rona, politely.

"That's true," the woman agreed, beaming as if Rona had paid the countryside a great compliment. "There you go now, before the milk gets warm. Come and see us any time, even if you don't want anything. You might see Wiri on your way home," she added. "He's around somewhere. He'll enjoy having someone his own age to play with."

Rona had her doubts. In her experience, boys couldn't be bothered with girls except to tease and pester them.

Pru the dog accompanied Rona as far as the gate where it collapsed with a sigh to resume its sleep.

THREE

At the bottom of the Thompsons' vegetable garden grew a gnarled old quince tree with a tangle of raspberry canes gone wild around its roots. Last year's fruit still hung on the branches, for no one could be bothered to pick it.

Perched high in the tree, Wiri watched the girl plodding home along the road to Shearwater. He had seen her arrive with the empty cans, now she was on the way back, looking around as she went.

He guessed his mother had told her to look out for him. Mum always seemed to think he was missing out on something, not having anyone his own age to mess around with. His older brothers and sister were practically grown up, Sissie was only four, and then there was the baby.

He turned his attention back to the book. It was slow work, puzzling out each line. It wasn't just that the lines were so cramped together that the words practically ran into each other. It was the writing itself. It had taken Wiri ages to realise that what looked like an 'f' was really an 's', and an 'r' looked like a 'v'.

The book was a diary, that much was obvious, and on the first page was a date — 1829. That was nearly two hundred years ago. The thought of holding in his hands something written by someone living all that time ago made his head swim. He even knew the man's name. It was Trevarren — and that was almost the same name as Mrs Varren's. There had to be a connection.

Wiri felt excited. He read again from the beginning.

My name is Jonathan Trevarren, Marriner, formerly Man of Devon, England, now Man of I know not Where. I have returned this day from my first Venture into Civilisation in more than one year with great

Treasure, namely this Book and ink wherewith to write in it.

Now I scarce know where to begin. In all the time since I arrived so unexpectedly upon the shores of this Land, I have had no occasion to use my Native Tongue except when addressing myself, which I confess I often did at first, being so much Alone. The only words of English I hear are those I utter myself. My new Wife laughs and runs away when I try to teach her my Language, seeing little use for it, but I will persevere, for when we have Children they must certainly learn their Father's tongue.

So for them, and for the Pleasure it gives me to practise the same, I mean to Write each day in this Book until I have told my whole Story. And, indeed, if I do not use my Language I fear I may forget it entirely.

My book will not be a Journal, for I have no longer any way of reckoning the Date, only the Sun to tell me of the passing days. I can say only that my Account begins in the middle part of December 1828 with Christmas not far off, turning the thoughts of the Crew towards home so that one and all of us (except perhaps Parry) wondered if we would see our Families in the new Year of Our Lord, 1829.

Wiri stopped and took a deep breath. He had to decide what to do with this. He was sure it was important, but if he took it home, the first thing that would happen was that his parents would take it off him —and he wanted to know what happened to Jonathan Trevarren. Everybody would say the diary was too valuable for a kid to have and they'd send it off to the museum or the university or somewhere for the experts to examine, and that would be the last he'd see of it.

No way, he thought. He'd keep it to himself for at least a few more days.

The billies full of milk were heavy and the wire handles cut into Rona's hands. She was glad when she reached the house at last.

She put the milk in the fridge. There did not seem to be much else to do except read and play with Mungo until Nan finally came down from the roof. Then they fed the hens together and collected the eggs.

While Nan prepared the meal, Rona set the table and took the peelings to the compost heap and fed the cat. After dinner she dried the dishes that Nan washed.

They did not talk much, and for Rona the long evening dragged. Nan was used to solitude. It did not occur to her that Rona might be bored. Rona, on the other hand, came to the conclusion that Nan did not want to be bothered with an unknown grandchild. The best she could do, she decided, was to be as little trouble as possible and hope that it wouldn't be too long before Mum came home. She smothered a yawn. She really was quite tired.

"You don't have to stay up if you'd like to go to bed," suggested Nan drily.

Rona jumped up. "I think I will," she said. "Goodnight then."

"Goodnight, Rona."

In her bedroom Rona looked at her unmade bed. That was something else she was going to have to do for herself. She had her shower and crawled between the untidy sheets.

The wind had come up again as darkness fell. Just as on the night before, Rona heard it sighing around the walls, but already she was growing used to it. Sleepily, she wondered if she would hear the bell again.

Rona was dreaming. She was deep underground, running through dark passages, looking for a bell that kept tolling — *dong, dong, dong* — shivering and echoing through her bones.

Sticky cobwebs wrapped themselves around her head. She fought to get clear of them —and woke with a start to hear the wind in the trees and the booming of the surf, but no bell. Had it been only in her dream? Or had it stopped as she woke?

Pushing aside the sheet that had draped itself over her face, she scrambled out of bed and pulled open the curtains. A bright, almost full moon rode above the rustling, restless garden. It edged with silver the roof of the hen-house and each shivering leaf on the trees. Paving stones gleamed like snow.

Rona caught her breath. Someone was out there, moving silently through the little gate. It was Nan; a black cloak pulled tightly around her against the tugging of the wind. She left the gate swinging and moved swiftly over the grass to the cliff top to look out over the sea, just as she had been doing when Rona and her mother had arrived.

Rona listened, but there was no sound from the bell. She must have imagined it, but she wondered what had woken Nan and sent her walking on the cliff in the middle of the night. Shyly, as if she had witnessed something private, Rona crept back to bed, but it was a long time before she slept again.

When she woke next it was to the shrill ringing of the telephone. Mum! She was out of bed instantly, but before she was halfway along the passage the ringing stopped and she heard Nan's voice.

"Yes . . . I see . . . of course . . . no . . . mmm . . ."

Rona fidgeted with impatience. Why didn't Nan

let her talk to Mum? Surely she wouldn't put the phone down without giving her a chance to speak — would she?

Finally, looking at Rona, Nan said, "Yes, she's right here. Hold on."

"Mum!" Rona shouted into the receiver.

"Hey! Not so loud! I can hear you just fine. How are you, sweetheart?" Mum could have been in the next room, she sounded so close.

"I'm okay. How's Dad? When are you coming home?"

"Dad's improving. He's responding to certain sounds, but he's not fully conscious yet. The doctors are optimistic though."

"But he will get better . . . "

"I hope so, darling. He'll be in hospital for quite a time, but you mustn't worry about him. I spend most of the day with him, talking to him and playing him music — I know he hears it — but we're going to have to be very patient, darling, all of us."

Rona swallowed the lump in her throat. "I will be, Mum. Tell Dad I love him. Shall I write to you?"

"You'd better! I've given Nan the address."

There was so much Rona wanted to say that she did not know how to start. While she was still thinking, Nan took a firm grip on the phone. "This will be costing your mother a fortune. Say goodbye now."

Rona just had time to yell, "Bye, Mum!" before the receiver was whisked away and her grandmother was also saying goodbye. Rona glowered at her. "I hadn't finished," she said, sullenly.

"Yes you had." Nan was unmoved. "All she needed was to know you're all right. Anything else you want, you can ask me."

They faced each other like opponents.

"What about pocket money?" muttered Rona.

"You don't need any here," Nan pointed out.

"I might want to buy some stamps and stuff to write to Mum."

"There are stamps and aerogrammes in the drawer there. Help yourself to what you need."

"What about school? I'll be missing heaps."

"If that worries you, you could have correspondence lessons like Wiri Thompson," said Nan, "but it's hardly worth arranging all that for such a short time. There are plenty of books here. Reading is the best education."

Rona was relieved to know that she was not going to have to start at a new school, but still cross with Nan for whipping away the phone so rapidly.

Nan appeared not to notice. "Set the table. We'll have breakfast," she said briskly.

After breakfast Nan said she had to finish painting the roof. "Later on I'll show you the best way down to the beach," she added. "In the meantime, I know you young folk like to be independent so I expect you can amuse yourself, can't you?"

I guess I'll have to, thought Rona. She nodded.

As Nan pulled on her overalls and hauled the can of paint up the ladder, Rona sighed. She missed Mum, missed her friends, even missed school. She really didn't have anyone to talk to, unless you counted Mungo — and he was asleep half the time.

Still in her pyjamas, Rona wondered what she should wear. Mum usually put out clean clothes for her, but Nan hadn't said anything about clothes. Most of them were still in her suitcase. Rona decided she'd better sort something out for herself. She put on clean underwear and a T-shirt and shorts, then put away the rest of her clothes in the dresser drawers. She gathered up the dirty garments and dumped them in the washing machine. She'd better check with Nan before starting the machine, she decided.

Next, she made her bed. It had been pretty uncomfortable last night, crawling into it with the bottom sheet all crumpled and the blankets twisted.

Back in the kitchen, she washed the dishes. Nan might not want her here, but at least she couldn't say she wasn't making herself useful. There did not seem to be anything else to do until she remembered the letter she had promised to write to Mum. She found the aerogrammes and made a start.

Rona filled half the page before deciding it was too glorious a day to be inside. The wind had gone, the sun was shining. She wanted to be doing something. She dropped her pen and ran outside.

Mungo was stalking something in the long grass just through the little brown gate. He crouched, his tail end swaying slowly, then faster and faster until, quick as a flash, he pounced. Rona vaulted the gate and ran after him, just in time to see him trotting away with a small grey mouse in his jaws.

She looked back at the house. Nan was out of sight on the far side of the roof. Now she was out here she might as well explore the place. She needn't go near the cliff edge, and in any case, it couldn't be that dangerous. Nan walked there. She had been standing there when they had arrived two days ago. Two days? It felt more like two weeks.

Wiri had had second thoughts. He had read more of the diary in bed last night. It was hard work, but exciting. He had found another name he recognised. It was too important to keep to himself.

"Mum," he said at breakfast, but she was heading towards the kitchen to top up the teapot.

"Eat up, Wiri," she said as she went.

"Dad? Dad. I've got something to —"

Dad leaned over to turn up the volume on the radio. "Hang on, I want to hear the weather."

"Are you going to eat that?" demanded Ricky.

Wiri fended off his brother's fork as it was about to spear a sausage off his plate. "Get off! Yes, I am. I'm trying to tell you something," he complained.

"Children should be seen and not heard," said his big sister, Maire.

"Pity no one told you that," Wiri muttered.

"Are we going to shift those sheep today, Dad?" Mark, the eldest brother asked. Dad heard that all right. Anything to do with the farm got his attention immediately.

"No one ever listens to me," Wiri moaned, but no one heard him. He grabbed the last slice of toast as his sister began to clear the table around him, rushing so she would not be late for work. She left, taking Ricky with her. They would be gone all day. Dad and Mark were outside the door, pulling on their boots. Sissie had quietly disappeared. That left Mum and the baby.

41

He tried again. "Mum . . . "

"Put these scraps in Pru's bowl for me please, Wiri," said Mum.

Wiri gave up. If they didn't want to know, he wouldn't bother trying to tell them.

Mrs Varren, he thought. She'd want to know about the names in the diary. But that girl was there now. Before he could decide what to do, his mother was reminding him about his schoolwork, hustling him away to his desk.

Rona looked down at the tiny beach. Ship Cove, Mum had called it. Gulls hung below her, freewheeling on the wind, and the waves rolled in endlessly from the sea, making her dizzy. It was true: there was no way down.

She remembered how the road curved close to the sea just before you reached the Thompsons' farm. It should be easy to get down to the beach at Sandy Bay from there. She set off.

Sure enough, there was just a low bank to climb down and soon she was slipping and sliding on the loose dry stones down to the sand, racing to the sea. She splashed through the cold waves, turned cartwheels on the sand and wrote her name in gigantic letters with a piece of driftwood.

Then, for luck, she wrote T-O-M. She looked

up to the sky and called out to whoever was listening: "Please make Dad get better quickly! Please!"

She couldn't bear then to look at Dad's name any longer and ran from it, leaving the magic to work, racing towards a long line of rocks that stretched out into the sea. Scrambling to the top to see what lay on the other side, Rona found that the beach continued, curving to another outcrop in the distance.

She jumped down and her feet sank deep into the wet sand. It was a small beach, but wonderful. It had everything: smooth, clean sand, rocks with small pools between them full of tiny crabs and anemones, a band of shells at the high tide mark. She galloped through the shallow water, kicking up her feet like a wild pony, splashing and leaping.

Her footprints on the sand were the only ones to be seen. Rona felt like the first person ever to have walked on it.

She looked up at the cliff. That must be Shearwater up there, she thought, recognising the dark, windswept trees. Of course, this was Varren's Bay. She would have passed the top of it on her way if she hadn't kept to the road. There must be a way down, if only Nan would show her.

Thinking of Nan reminded Rona that she had been gone for some time. She had better get back

. . . but when she turned around, everything looked different. The barrier of rocks was shorter. Huge waves were breaking over it, flinging a froth of white spray high into the air.

She had forgotten about the tide coming in!

The place where she had earlier climbed over the rocks was now under water. She would have to get over the steeper rocks at the foot of the cliff. At first she was not worried, but as she got closer she found that the rocks were smoother and higher than she had realised. Nowhere could she find a foothold or anything to pull herself up by.

The tide was still rising. Big rollers broke with a roar on the sand and galloped towards her. Rona backed up, but a line of seaweed and the crunch of shells under her feet warned her that the water came right up to the cliff.

She was in big trouble.

FOUR

Sissie watched her mother feed the baby. Afterwards, Mum patted his back until he brought up a noisy, milky burp.

"That's rude," said Sissie.

Mum laughed. "Not when you're as little as Bub." She tucked him into his stroller, which had been made into a flat bed, and wheeled it onto the verandah. He was already asleep.

Sissie wasn't surprised. He had been yelling half the night, keeping them all awake. They'd had him for six weeks now and all he did was feed, sleep, poo and yell.

When Mum had said they were going to have a new baby, Sissie had been excited. A little brother or sister to play with, they'd said, but how could you play with this screaming thing? She wished she could send him back where he came from.

Well, why not? Auntie Pat said the fairies had left him in the flax, like Moses in the bulrushes, for Mum and Dad to find. Dad said that was silly, and Bub had grown in Mum's tummy, but Sissie thought she would rather believe Auntie Pat.

Carefully, so as not to wake him, she lifted the baby out of his pram and carried him down the verandah steps. He just fitted into her doll's pram. She wrapped the blanket around him so he would not get cold waiting for the fairies to collect him, and set off.

In his room, Wiri printed THE END in large red letters at the bottom of the page, closed the folder and shoved it thankfully into the drawer. Done it, he thought. The rest of the day was his. Now he could go and see Mrs Varren.

He wrapped the precious book in a plastic bag and placed it carefully in his backpack.

From his bedroom window he could see Sissie. Where was she off to? he wondered. And what was that in her toy pram? Suddenly suspicious, he hitched the straps of the pack over his shoulders and ran downstairs.

Mum was hanging out washing in the yard. The stroller on the verandah was empty. Full of curiosity now, he tracked his little sister. If the baby looked like coming to harm he would take him off her and return him to his bed.

The baby was heavier than he looked. By the time Sissie reached the paddock her arms were aching from pushing the pram over the rough ground, and the flax was in the furthest corner of the paddock, by the dam. She lifted Bub out of the pram and sat down to rest with the baby on her lap. He had woken up and was staring at her with wide-open eyes.

Nearby, a cow was acting strangely. It bellowed and strained. Perhaps it had eaten something bad, Sissie thought. She had better keep an eye on it in case she had to fetch Dad or Mark to see to it.

Something was happening at its back end. There was a sudden slithering movement and something dropped out onto the grass. As Sissie stared, she saw it was a calf, already trying to struggle to its feet, looking around in amazement at this strange new place it had suddenly found itself in. The cow began to lick it clean.

On Sissie's lap the baby wriggled. Sissie lifted him to her face and licked his cheek and his little blob of a nose. "Moo," she said. "You can be my calf."

Bub made a funny gurgling sound and all his arms and legs seemed to be moving at once. As Sissie held him tightly, afraid she was going to drop him, he smiled.

It was his very first smile —apart from when he was sleeping, and Mum always said that was wind. All the family had tried to make him smile but this was his first . . . and it had been for her. She couldn't wait to tell Mum. And about the calf.

Wiri watched until she reached the house. He saw Mum come out and take the baby from Sissie, then all three went inside and he headed off towards Shearwater.

Mrs Varren was still on the roof but she had almost finished painting it. It was no hardship for Wiri to wait on the cliff above Ship Cove. It was warm up here in the sun, his back propped against a heap of old timber that might once have been a shed. Now it was almost invisible under a blanket of windblown soil and grass.

He took out the diary and read again the page he had read in bed last night.

I will not dwell on the Voyage of our Vessel up to that time. Suffice it to say that the 'Shearwater' was a tidy Ship of some 550 tons, properly equipped and provisioned for our long Journey.

We cast off from Plymouth Dock on a fine May morning with much Hope, to great cheering and weeping and waving of handkerchiefs by those on shore, all knowing it would be many long Months, even Years, before they next saw their Loved Ones.

Had I known then that none of those brave Men would see their Homes again I would not have felt so downcast that I had no Mother or Sister to send me off with a kiss. On the contrary, now I am glad that there is none to mourn me on olde England's shores, my Family having all passed away before I left.

She was a sweet, sound Ship, the 'Shearwater', and we made good time carrying our Cargo of much-needed supplies to the Convict Settlement of Kingston on Norfolk Island, a Hellhole if ever there was one. We loaded up with wool and wood, tall straight pines for Ships' masts, and sailed for home, making West along the Southern Coast of Australia.

We were still within sight of Land when we discovered we had on Board a Stowaway —

Wiri looked up. Was that someone shouting? He listened, but heard nothing more. Must have been a seagull, he decided. He read on.

—as evil-looking a Character as you could imagine, much scarred across his back from the Terrible Beatings inflicted on the poor Wretches in that place. Whatever his crime, and he was no Innocent, we agreed he had paid his Penalty. Furthermore, the Captain was unwilling to lose the tide and another day by turning back, so he signed him on as a Crew Member under the name of Abel Parry.

Another wave broke over Rona's feet, swirling greedily around her ankles, and she screamed as she felt herself starting to slip. She leaned into the cliff in a desperate effort to keep her balance.

Terrified, she had hauled herself up onto a boulder but there was no place higher to go. Her nails were torn and her fingers raw from scrabbling at the cliff face, but there was nothing to grip on to. All she could do now was hope the tide would turn before it dragged her down.

She screamed again as the next wave crashed against the boulder, reaching her knees ...

Wiri sat up. Someone *was* shouting —screaming,

actually — in a real panic about something. Dropping his book, he took off along the cliff top in the direction the noise had come from. It wouldn't be the first time a stranger to the area had climbed over the rocks to Varren's Bay at low tide, only to find themselves trapped when the tide came in.

Then he saw her — the girl who was staying with Mrs Varren. It was a good job she hadn't made the mistake of trying to swim out around the end of the barrier. The treacherous current would have swept her away for sure.

Most days, if she stayed where she was she would be safe, but only yesterday Wiri's Dad had warned them all not to take the boat out fishing because of the extra high tides forecast. He had better get her off the beach quickly.

Rona heard him before she saw him, a thin cry carried on the wind.

"Hey, girl! Over here!"

Turning her head sideways, she saw the boy from the farm, Wiri. He was waving at her from a ledge a little way up the cliff.

"Come on!" he yelled. "Come up here!"

"Where? How do I get up there?"

He came lower. "I'll show you, but come on!"

Rona looked at the water gurgling around the boulder, took a deep breath, jumped and ran. She got splashed from head to foot but the water here was only up to her knees as yet. She thrashed and stumbled her way through the bubbling surf to where Wiri stood, urging her on. It wasn't until she had almost reached him that she could see the path carved into the cliff.

"Come on — up here." Wiri grabbed her hand and pulled her up the first few steps to safety. Rona clung to the iron handrail, wondering how she could have missed seeing it.

"Thanks," she gasped. "I thought I was going to drown."

"Nah," he said nonchalantly, but he knew the danger had been real. "Better not come down here again until you know your way around, eh?"

She nodded.

"You okay now?" She looked very pale to Wiri.

"Yeah, sure," she said. "Is this the way up?"

Relieved that she wasn't going to fuss or go faint on him, Wiri led the way to the top.

"Thanks," she said again as they collapsed onto the firm, dry grass. "Lucky you heard me."

"I was coming to see Mrs Varren, to show her something. She's up on the roof, so I was sitting up here waiting for her to come down."

Rona shivered and got to her feet. Her clothes were wet, and gritty sand clung to her legs.

"I'd better go and get cleaned up. Do you want to come and see Nan now?"

"No." Wiri shook his head. "I'll come back later."

Rona looked down at the beach. It had been so beautiful down there at first. "Will you show me the safe places to go?" she asked. "Nan's always busy."

"Sure."

"Well, I'd better go," Rona repeated. Then she heard it again. The echoing chimes that she had heard in the night. She stared down at the ground beneath her feet. The sound was coming from below them! Quickly she looked down at Wiri. There was no doubt about it; he could hear it too.

His eyes met hers. "It's the ghost bell," he whispered.

"What ghost bell?" Rona dropped to her knees beside him. "Nan said it was just the wind, but it's not, is it?"

"I've never heard it before," said Wiri. "People tell stories about it and that's all I thought it was — just a story. It's bad luck, they reckon."

"What kind of bad luck?"

Wiri was reluctant to explain, but when Rona pressed him he continued: "They say when the bell rings, someone's going to die. I don't reckon that's true," he added quickly, "but that's what they say."

Dad! thought Rona. "That's silly!" she cried angrily. "How can hearing a bell mean anything! Where is it, anyway?"

"I don't know. No one knows."

"Hasn't anybody looked for it?"

" 'Course they have. They just can't find it."

"How come you've never heard it before?" Rona asked.

"You can't hear it from our house. Shearwater is the only place it's ever been heard. Don't get your knickers in a knot about it —I told you it probably isn't true."

"I'm not!" protested Rona. She shivered again and this time it wasn't only her damp clothes that sent a chill through her. "I'd better go. See you later?"

"Okay," said Wiri, as Rona ran off.

At the house, Rona slowed. Stupid bell, she thought. I won't even think about it. Aware of her messy state, she removed her shoes at the door, but her feet were nearly as bad. She wondered if she could slip in without Nan seeing her.

The kitchen was empty. She crept along the passage, passing the lounge, Nan's bedroom and the spare room safely. The studio door was open, and there was Nan, working on a piece of bone. Rona flitted past on tiptoe to her own room where she stripped off her wet things. When she was clean and dry, she strolled casually into the studio.

"Ah, there you are," Nan said. "I was beginning to think I'd have to send out a search party."

"Sorry," said Rona.

"No need to be," said Nan. "Just so long as you stay out of trouble. I didn't wait lunch. Help yourself to whatever you want."

Rona moved closer. "What are you making?"

"It's a sea horse." Nan showed her. "I like the way their tails curl."

Rona touched the smooth, creamy bone with her finger. "It's beautiful. Did you make that one you're wearing? The seagull?"

"Oh no, that's very old. It's been in the family for years," Nan replied. "And it's not a gull. It's a shearwater."

"Is the house named after a bird? I've never even heard of a shearwater," said Rona.

"Look it up. There's a book about seabirds in the bookcase."

Rona wanted to tell Nan about hearing the bell again, but she felt Nan would only brush her off and say it was the wind or something. Instead she said, "I met Wiri Thompson. He's coming to show you something this afternoon."

"Mm?" said Nan, concentrating on her work. Rona took herself off to find something to eat.

Wiri was late for lunch. As he slipped into his chair, he said: "Hey, you'll never guess what!"

"Hands," said Mum. He sighed and went to wash them.

"I heard the bell," he announced loudly as he sat down again. No one paid any attention. "Up at Shearwater. The ghost bell. That girl heard it too."

Now they were listening. "Wiri, are you making this up?" Mum demanded.

"No way! Honest! I'm not," he protested indignantly.

"'Course he is," scoffed Mark. "Everyone knows there's no bell really."

"There is too!" Wiri yelled.

"That'll do," said Mum.

Sissie was bored. "Can I get down?" she whined.

"All right, off you go then," Mum said.

Sissie skipped out of the room. She saw Wiri's bag on the floor and picked it up, swinging it from side to side. "Ding-dong-bell," she sang.

Mum said quietly, "The Shearwater Bell. Your dad heard it once. Tell them, Dev."

Wiri stared at her. Shearwater again. A house, a ship and now a bell.

"It was a long time ago. I was just a kid," his father said, leaning back in his chair. "There was a huge storm and some of us went up on the cliff to watch for the fishing boats," he said slowly. "I remember standing there, and all of a sudden there was this spooky donging sound all around us. Couldn't tell where it came from, any of us."

He paused. No one moved as they waited for him to go on.

"The wind blew up out of nowhere, caught the boats by surprise. They all got back safely except one. One went down. Josh Varren and two crew were lost."

"Varren?" said Mark. "Mrs Varren's husband?"

"Yes," said Mum. "I remember that. She was left with a little girl to bring up. Rona's mother."

"You heard the bell and someone died!" Wiri was excited. "It really is bad luck then."

"Nah," said Dad. "Just superstition. It was a freak wave as they tried to come in over the bar. Nothing to do with any bell. It's always been a dangerous coast for ships."

As Wiri opened his mouth to ask more, out of the corner of his eye he saw Sissie. The diary had fallen out of his bag and now she was sitting on the floor, flicking the pages over carelessly, pretending to read. He leaped from the table and snatched it from her. Already one brittle page had torn. Sissie gave a roar of fury.

"Wiri!" cried his mother. "What are you doing?"

"It's mine!" he protested. "She's always spoiling my things."

"Just what your big brothers used to say about you when you were four," she reminded him. "If you don't want Sissie to touch your things, put them away."

"It was in my bag!" Wiri muttered, wrapping up the book again. The sooner he took it to Mrs Varren the better.

FIVE

Rona had taken her grandmother's advice and was reading *Seabirds of the World* when she heard Wiri tapping on the back door. She let him in.

"What are you reading?" he asked.

She showed him the full-page illustration of a bird in flight. It was black on top, white underneath, with a strong pointed black beak and long narrow wings.

"Are you into bird-watching?" Wiri asked.

"No — it's a shearwater. Nan wears a bone carving

of one round her neck," Rona explained. "It's really old. She — what's the matter?" There was an odd expression on Wiri's face.

"A shearwater! I thought that was just a name. I didn't know it was a bird!" he cried.

"Me neither," said Rona, and she read aloud the caption beneath the picture: " 'Many of those seen around the coast of Britain in the summer go halfway across the world in winter to South America. A few may even reach Australia or New Zealand.' "

" 'They cover vast distances in an almost effortless gliding flight, sometimes swooping so low that the tips of their wings actually shear the waves,' " read Nan over Rona's shoulder, startling both children, who had not heard her come in.

"Doesn't that make it a wonderful name for a ship?" she went on. "Imagine a full-rigged sailing ship, skimming over the waves, crossing the ocean to the other side of the world."

"A ship?" repeated Rona. "Was there a ship called the *Shearwater*?"

"Apparently," said Nan before Wiri could tell what he knew. "This place was called Shearwater after a vessel said to have been wrecked off Ship Cove many years ago."

"That's the bell we heard!" Wiri blurted out.

Nan hesitated, then said calmly, "Yes, the story goes that the bell belonged to the *Shearwater.*"

"Did it go down with the ship?" asked Rona. "It could be ringing under the water."

"No, there's no trace of any wreck," Nan said. "Many divers have searched for it but there's nothing there."

"A ghost bell," said Wiri with a shiver.

Nan shook her head. "I don't think so," she said, then changed the subject. "Rona said you had something to show me, Wiri."

Wiri dumped his backpack on the table and drew out the parcel. He unwrapped the book and put it into Mrs Varren's hands, then stood back and waited for her to say something.

"Mrs Varren?" he said at last. She had been looking through the book in silence for some time.

She started. "Oh! I'm sorry, Wiri. I'm just — stunned. This is extraordinary. Have you any idea what you've got here?"

"An old diary, I think," he answered.

"Yes. That is exactly what it is. Where on earth did you find this, Wiri?"

"Under the floorboards in a cupboard in my bedroom."

Rona had been puzzling over the spidery scrawl. "Can you read it, Wiri? I can't make it out at all."

"Yep," said Wiri. "It's hard, but it gets easier as you go — once you've worked out that things that look like f's are s's and stuff like that."

Nan turned the book over in her hands. "Well, I'll be! Amazing! It's in remarkably good condition, considering its age. You must show it to someone who knows about these things. I can phone the museum for you if you like."

Wiri looked uncomfortable. He didn't want some expert taking his book over. He'd probably never see it again.

"Don't you want to?" asked Rona. "Why not?"

He shrugged. It was hard to explain.

"So how did you come to find it?" asked Nan.

"I was looking for a place to hide stuff where Sissie wouldn't find it, and there was this loose floorboard in the cupboard. The book was underneath."

"Just lying there? Not in a box or with any other things?" Nan questioned him.

"No. The cupboard's built into the wall and I reckon it must've fallen down the back of the shelf and through the floor — years ago probably, 'coz the original shelves have been replaced."

"Incredible," Nan murmured. "Looks like a mouse has had a nibble at this corner, but basically it's hardly damaged at all. I see the end pages are missing.

The last one appears to end in mid-sentence. Probably someone tore them out to use at some time. Mmm . . . this looks like a more recent tear."

"Sissie," said Wiri grimly.

"See? If you keep it at home, sooner or later it will be damaged again. If this is a diary, it will be an invaluable account of life nearly two hundred years ago."

Wiri pulled a face and nodded. He knew she was right.

Rona, handling the book as if it were made of eggshells, had returned to the first page. It was confusing, the way the writer used capital letters when it wasn't a new sentence, but she was beginning to make out some of the words now. She gasped. "Nan! Listen! 'My Name is Jonathan Trevarren —', then there's something I can't read . . . but Nan! Trevarren! It's almost like your name."

"I wonder," Nan murmured. "So long ago . . . the name could have been shortened over the years. That happens sometimes."

"This Jonathan Trevarren could have been your great-great — goodness knows how many greats — grandfather!" Rona cried. "Mine too!"

"Then what was it doing in our house?" demanded Wiri.

"Good question," said Nan.

"Can we read it?" asked Rona.

Wiri picked up the book and held it close to his chest.

Nan looked at him thoughtfully. "That's for Wiri to decide," she said quietly. "It's his book."

"Do you really think it's valuable?" Wiri asked Nan.

"Its value is in the information it holds. I doubt if it would bring you a fortune if you sold it, but to anyone interested in the past, its loss would be tragic."

Rona and her grandmother waited to see what the boy would do.

"If I promise to keep it safe," asked Wiri, "will you promise not to tell anyone else about it until I'm ready?"

"All right," agreed Nan. "Sounds fair enough. Where will you keep it?"

"Could I keep it here?"

Nan nodded. "If you like."

"And I can come and read it and find out what it says?"

"Any time you want."

"Thanks." Wiri looked at Rona. "You can read it too if you like, 'coz it could be about your family . . . but you're not allowed to tell anyone about it."

"Who would I tell?" she asked. "But thanks anyway."

Nan found a soft, clean cloth. "Keep it wrapped in this," she said. "Don't let it get damp, and wash your hands before you handle it."

Later, Rona asked Wiri why he was so anxious not to share the book with his family. He tried to explain, and she could see that it must be difficult to keep anything to yourself when you were one of a big family, especially when most of them were older than you. "It would just disappear off to some museum for the experts to look at and I bet no one would even bother to tell me what was in it," he said.

They were sitting at the table in Rona's room with the book open between them. She had brought in a second chair and pulled the table close to the window to get the best possible light while they tried to decipher the crabby writing.

"They'll take it eventually," said Rona. "We should write out a copy to keep."

Wiri groaned. "I hate writing."

"I don't. I like it," said Rona. She found an almost empty school exercise book, turned to a clean page and began. *My name is Jonathan Trevarren,* she wrote. "Oh, what *is* that next word? You can't have two v's together."

"Can too — what about rewed?" said Wiri. "Anyway, they're not v's, they're r's. It's 'marriner'. He was a sailor."

"Well, what's this word?"

"Venture. Look, don't worry about writing it down. It'd take forever. I want to find out what happened with Abel Parry."

"Who?"

"A stowaway. I'd better tell you the story so far."

"All right. I can copy out the pages we've read after you've gone home . . . if you like."

Wiri thought about it quickly and nodded. It would be good to have their own record of Jonathan Trevarren's diary and if Rona would do the work, so much the better. He brought her up to date and read on.

Leaving the Coast of Australia behind, we headed North to make our last Port of Call (and it was indeed to be our Last) on the Island of Java. From there we would make for Home, rounding Cape Horn on the way, which filled some of the Crew with Dread, while others took Delight in telling Tales of its Horrors to the Greenhorns who had not sailed that Ocean before.

In Java we filled our remaining Hold with Chests of Spice. Here too we took aboard a Passenger. A Mr Bullivant boarded with much Baggage, accompanied by a Black Servant dressed all in white who carried a heavy, brass-bound Box.

This Box became the subject of much Gossip and Speculation among the Crew for it was never left unguarded for a single minute of the Day or Night. When Mr Bullivant strolled on Deck or took his meals with the Captain, his servant Ahmed remained in the Cabin with it, only seeking his own Sustenance when his Master returned. At night Ahmed slept on the Floor outside the cabin door — and mightily uncomfortable he must have been when the Ship rolled and tossed in a High Sea.

It was Abel Parry who uncovered the Secret. He had made himself useful in the Galley and proved to be so Capable that before long he had taken over as Cook. Now he befriended Ahmed, preparing special meals for him as it was against the Black Man's Religion to eat Pork or Pig Meat of any kind.

They were an oddly-matched Pair: Parry scarred, pale and pinched; the Black Man in his spotless white Tunic. Each evening, when Parry brought Ahmed his plate, he would sit by him while he ate and they would talk, each in his own Language, but seeming to understand the other well enough.

At last Parry achieved what I believe had been his Object all along. He persuaded Ahmed to show him the Contents of the Box. The Rumour had long since spread that it was full of Treasure, Mr Bullivant's life Savings after years of Trading in the East. And *so it was. For once, Rumour told the Truth. I saw it Myself. But that was later. At the time we had only Parry's account, which lost nothing in the telling.*

Gold coins stacked in piles of ten were held in place by Bars of Silver.

"Treasure!" Rona could not contain her excitement. "I guessed it was," Wiri grinned. He continued.

Beside them soft cloth bags containing uncut Gems: Diamonds in one, Rubies in another, Sapphires, Emeralds, Pearls too, in a long string, and rings and neck chains of Gold, a single link worth more than I possessed in all the World.

Mr Bullivant kept one Key to the Box. Ahmed wore another around his Neck. For days Parry tried to discover a way of getting that Key, but it would have done him no good for he was never alone with the Box. He turned his mind to more sinister methods. Instead of merely hoping to steal a Gold Coin or two, he now began to covet the whole Treasure. I truly believe the Sight of such Riches had made him crazy, for he began to urge the Crew to seize the Chest.

"There's enough and to spare, lads," I heard him say. "Share and share alike, equal for all. We'll be as rich as Lords. No more salt pork and hard tack, but ale every night and a warm bed ashore."

None would listen at first, but like Water dripping on a Stone, he wore the weaker ones down. When they protested that should they be caught they would be Hanged for sure, he laughed at their Fears. "Not if we take the Ship, maties," he told them. "We'll change her Name and sail to the Islands, sell her, take our split and go our ways. Pay your passage Home in style if that be your Wish, or make for the Colonies and buy some Land if you fancy the Life of a Farmer or a Storekeeper."

We had been eighteen months from Home by then and the men were weary of the Ship, the maggotty meat and weevil-infested biscuit, wet clothes and never-ending Work. Once Home they would soon forget the discomfort and be hankering to sail again, but at that moment it was easy to tempt them with Dreams of Luxury. I was sorely tempted myself but did not believe it possible to carry out his Plan without Harm to Innocent people.

"We'll put the Cap'n and Bullivant ashore someplace where they'll soon be rescued along with any Man who don't care to join us," Parry promised. "All we need is time to disappear."

Thus his Plan was hatched. And now I must confess my own Guilt. Had I gone directly to the Captain and told him all I knew, Parry would have been clapped in Irons and the tragic Events which later occurred

would have been avoided. I would not be here and
my Shipmates would still be living.

But Alas, hoping some other Man would reveal the
Evil Plan, I resolved to wait until Parry was ready
to act before I spoke out. I delayed too long and by
holding my Tongue I condemned them all to Death.
The Guilt of my Silence will haunt me all my Days.

"Wow!" said Rona. This was exciting stuff —
and it was all true! It had really happened. "Keep
going, Wiri," she urged.

Wiri had been reading slowly, pausing to work out
words that had been blotted or when the handwriting
became too difficult to decipher. Now his throat
was dry.

"I need a break," he said.

SIX

Rona brought glasses of fruit juice from the kitchen and a handful of biscuits. From the window she could see Nan working in the garden, so they were not likely to be interrupted for a while yet.

Soon Wiri was ready to carry on.

We were sailing in Fair Weather in the Western Pacific seas when Parry considered he had enough Support to carry out his evil intention. Every man of the

Crew was approached and forced to choose For or Against. Those for Parry were armed with Knives and Staves. Those against him were bundled below Decks with the Hatches battened down. They put up little resistance, being much afraid of Parry and believing that the Captain and Officers would soon subdue him and release them. As Prisoners they would be in no Danger of being accused of siding with him.

As for me, the Second Mate, I was unaware of what Parry was about. I had been on Watch and was asleep in my bunk. I woke to feel the cold muzzle of a Pistol pressed against my throat and looked up to see Parry's mean eyes staring into mine. "What's it to be, Jonathan Trevarren?" he whispered. "A share of the Gold or a cold swim?"

Then I knew for sure what he had planned. I realised I had suspected it all along but like a Fool had shut my eyes to it. "You'll hang," I told him.

"They'll never catch me," he boasted. "Or at least I'll live like a King till they do, not like a bilge rat!"

"You can't sail the ship without the Officers," I reminded him. "You'll run her aground on the first Reef you come to."

"Then help us and save your Shipmates," he hissed in my face, and even as I recoiled from his foul breath it came to me that if I appeared to go along with him I might yet be able to do some Good.

"I never much cared for cold water," I told him and he laughed. He watched me dress and followed me to the Wheelhouse, the Pistol held to my back along the Way. The man at the Helm looked at me nervously.

"Where's the Captain?" I asked. "And the Passengers?"

"Below," Parry replied.

"And the Mate?"

"Below," he repeated, and the man at the Wheel gave a whinny like a frightened Horse. Later I understood the meaning of that laugh.

Wiri stopped reading and looked at Rona. She stared back at him, wide-eyed. A shiver ran up her spine. This was just like the Bounty mutiny, she thought.

It is painful to write more. I will tell my Tale as briefly as I may. I have some skill in reading Charts and under my Direction we followed the Course set by the Captain.

Meanwhile, the loyal Crew grew restless under the hatches. Parry brought them up on Deck and now we heard of a new Plan he had formed. I learned too of the fate of the Captain, the Officers, Mr Bullivant and even poor Ahmed. They had gone Below, right enough, to the bottom of the Ocean. We were offered a Choice: to join them or to sail with Parry in his

73

new Role as Buccaneer. For so he had decided. Our good Ship 'Shearwater' was to become a Pirate Ship.

It was no Choice. Better to stay Alive and escape when we could, than meet certain Death in Waters infested with I know not what monstrous Creatures.

The Crew were divided. Those who followed Parry willingly were set to watch those of us serving him perforce. We were kept apart in separate Watches so there was never the chance to unite and overcome the Villain. To tempt us further he showed us the Casket of Jewels, promising us all a part of it. "We'll share it fair and square among all who pull their weight," he declared. "I'll keep it Safe for you, lads, never fear."

So the Treasure remained in the Cabin once occupied by poor Bullivant, now taken over by Abel Parry. I had little Faith that we would see much of it in any Shareout, nor had I any wish to Profit from another man's Death.

"Turn her head West, Trevarren," he ordered me. "Forget Cape Horn. Take her back to the Spice Islands and the Chinee Sea."

Parry had determined to make the China Sea his base, dreaming of rich hauls of Silks, Spices, Camphor Wood, Tiger Skins and Ivory.

Is it my fancy, or did the 'Shearwater' herself hate her new role? It seemed to me that she sailed less freely and resisted turning back from the wide Pacific. The Weather, too, conspired against us. It was November,

Spring in these Southern Latitudes, and in the Seas we now sailed it was the Season for Typhoons.

Strong hot winds from the North buffeted us, driving us off Course. Thrown here and there by Great Waves, blinded by lashing rain day after day, I was not able to log our Progress or calculate our Bearing. All I knew was that we were being blown further and further South, a fact that became clear to us all as the Weather grew colder, the rain more stinging.

And then an even mightier Storm struck us. As Night fell the Wind screamed through the rigging as if a Thousand Devils were taunting us — or the Ghosts of our murdered Shipmates. Waves picked the Ship up bodily and dropped her into Troughs so deep we feared she would never come up again. Time and again she rolled until we were certain she could never right herself, yet somehow she stayed afloat.

The Crew were lashed to their Bunks, I to the Wheel with 2 men at my side. But we could not hold her. All was Blackness and Fury and unimaginable Noise. In the midst of it all a mighty Crack shuddered through the Timbers of the 'Shearwater' and the wheel spun in our hands. The Storm had broken her back and we were drifting aimlessly. She was Doomed, but as if it had done its Worst the Wind now seemed to ease somewhat, though still blowing Mightily. We clung on, Praying that we'd live to see another day.

At last the Terrible Night ended. As blackness turned to grey we looked out over a still heaving Sea and saw Land. We glimpsed it only from the Peaks, losing Sight of it as we dropped into the Troughs, but we were drifting Closer. Soon it was Visible all the time and the men began to Cheer (those who had Survived, for 3 had died from injury or been lost overboard). I, however, was filled with Foreboding as I looked at the jagged black Rocks of that savage Coastline. Huge waves crashed down onto the Shore. The Wind and Tide carried us with them and I knew that once the 'Shearwater' struck those vicious Rocks it would be only a matter of Minutes before she Broke up.

A mast snapped above our heads. It fell across the Deck in a tangle of rigging, grazing my brow. Parry screamed that the Ship was breaking up and Urged the Men to Swim for it. In vain I shouted my Warnings. But alas, the Men followed him like Sheep. They leaped into the seething Tide, discovering too Late the Power of the waves. Like Twigs in a Torrent, the Men were tossed Helplessly against the Rocks. I clung to the Wheel and Wept as I saw dark heads and Desperate arms rise briefly then disappear Forever. Every Man was Lost.

Rona felt a tightening in her chest and a prickling behind her eyes. The knowledge that this was written from first-hand experience made it seem so much worse. Those poor souls, she thought.

I alone was Left when the Ship stopped with a jolt that threw me across the Deck, half stunning me. The 'Shearwater' was Impaled on an outcrop of Rock some few yards from Land, but it might as well have been a Hundred Miles for all the Chance I stood of swimming Ashore in that Sea. I sank to my knees. There was Blood on my hands from the cut on my Head but that was of little Concern to me now. Waves hammered the Vessel, tearing timbers out of her side where she was Holed. Rigging and Spars were ripped away around me. I cowered under the fallen mast for Protection and Prayed to the Lord for Salvation. A wooden grating skidded across the Deck. As it came within reach I seized it and pulled it to me.

The Tide was at its fullest, ready to turn and now, with uncanny Suddenness, the Wind dropped completely. The shrieking overhead ceased, though the thunder and boom of the Waves and the cracking and grinding of the Ship on the Rocks was unending. She settled lower, and still I waited. It may have been an Hour, I could not tell, before I felt the Deck lift under my feet. Then I threw myself onto the grating and when the next wave washed over me I let go the Mast and went with it.

*Battered, beaten and bloody, deafened and half-drowned,
I was hurled onto the Shore of this Island which I
now know to be the North Island of New Zealand.
At that moment, however, I knew Nothing. I lost all
Consciousness, sprawled face down on a tiny patch of
yellow sand, the only Beach among those Rocks. Such
was my good Fortune. There I lay while the Tide receded
and I did not revive until it began to return, lapping
around my legs. I staggered to my feet, amazed to discover
I was still Alive. Why I alone should have been
Saved I could not say, but as I gave Thanks I vowed
that for the rest of my Life I would seek to do only
Good.*

Rona drew a deep breath and came back to the
present as Wiri's voice slowed and stopped. "Wow,"
she breathed.

"Yeah," he agreed. He looked around as if surprised
to see where he was. "I wonder what the time is?"
he said, checking his watch.

It was later than either of them had imagined.
"Oh blast!" he cried. "I should've brought the cows
in for milking ages ago. I'd better get a move on."

"What about the book?" Rona reminded him.

Wiri wrapped it carefully in the cloth and Rona
put it in an empty drawer in the dresser.

"I'll write out the story as far as we've read tonight,"

she told him. "It'll be something to do. Can I tell Nan what we've read?"

"Okay, but don't read any more," Wiri warned. "It's my book and I want to be the one who reads it first. Okay?"

"Okay, no problem." Rona was dying to know what happened next, but knew it wouldn't be fair to read on without Wiri. "You coming tomorrow?"

"Soon as I can," said Wiri. "I'll have to do my schoolwork in the morning, but after that I can come. See ya!"

He rushed away, calling goodbye to Mrs Varren as he went.

As he raced up the track to the farmhouse, Sissie came dancing out to meet him. "You didn't bring the cows in," she chanted. "Mum and me had to do it and now you have to do the dishes instead, Mum says."

"I don't care," Wiri told her. "I had something more important than cows to do," but he wouldn't tell her what.

Wiri washed the dishes that evening without a murmur, his mind reliving the account of the Shearwater shipwreck. He wanted to discover how Jonathan Trevarren had survived. And what happened to the treasure? Had it gone down with the ship?

Tomorrow he might find out.

SEVEN

Rona and Nan were having breakfast the next morning when the telephone rang. Nan nodded. "You get it," she said.

"Is it Mum?" Rona asked.

"Well you won't find out sitting there, will you?" said Nan and Rona rushed to the phone before Nan could change her mind.

"Hello, sweetie-pie!" It was Mum all right.

"Hi Mum. How's Dad? Is he going to be all right?"

"He's . . . well, he's not so good, to be honest. But you mustn't worry, love, he's in the best of hands." Mum was trying not to sound anxious, but Rona knew her too well to be fooled.

"He *is* going to get better, isn't he?" She had to ask, even while dreading the answer. "Say he is, Mum. Promise."

She heard her mother draw a long breath. "Oh Rona, I can't make promises like that. You wouldn't want me to lie to you, would you?"

"No, I suppose not. Just promise to tell me if anything happens."

"Of course I will, darling, and remember — the doctors and nurses are all doing everything they can. I can't tell you more than that. I'll call again soon, love."

"I've written you a letter," said Rona.

"Oh, that'll be lovely, darling. I'll read it to Dad when it arrives. There are flickers —moments when he seems about to wake up — especially when I'm talking about you."

"Wish I could talk to him myself," Rona said sadly.

"I know, love. But I'm with him all day and they've found me a bed in the nurses' hostel so I can sleep close by. People have been so kind. And you're sure you're all right?"

"Yes, Nan's looking after me." Nan was making

signals at her. "Hang on, she wants to speak to you, I think. Give Dad a kiss from me. Bye."

She handed the receiver to Nan and heard her reassuring her daughter that Rona was well and happy.

"Keeping busy, at any rate," she said. "I hardly saw her yesterday." That was true enough.

Later that morning, Rona copied out some more of the diary. She had done some the evening before, but it took far longer than she had expected.

There were other things to do, too. Nan showed her how to start the washing machine so that at last she would have some clean clothes. Then she had to hang them out to dry. She had her bed to make, the hens to feed and the eggs to collect, and Nan reminded her that she had not fetched any milk the day before. Rona suspected that Nan was deliberately keeping her busy to stop her worrying about her dad. It helped a little.

"I'll go and get the milk after lunch," she offered, "then Wiri might be able to come back with me."

"Just as you like," Nan agreed. "Come along — I'll show you where the path down to the beach starts."

Rona could not tell her that she had already been up it, if not down, without giving away her narrow escape of the day before.

"Take care, and use the handrail," Nan told her. "I'm not going to fuss over you, but we don't want any accidents."

"What's this?" Rona ran towards the overgrown heap of timber.

"Probably an old long-drop dunny, or even a well," Nan said. "It was already covered up long before my time."

"Why is it fenced off?"

"To keep sheep — and nosy people like you, miss — from falling in," said her grandmother. "Come on. Let's have lunch."

Wiri had spent the morning doing his schoolwork with his mother's help. Sissie sat at the table, too, drawing and making little books that she then 'read' to them.

By the time Rona came for the milk, he was ready to go back with her.

"Make sure you're home in time for milking," his mother warned.

Rona managed to put aside her worries about her father — at least for the moment — and was eager to continue reading the diary.

It took only a few minutes to search that tiny Beach and to satisfy myself that I was indeed the only Survivor.

Then I stumbled over the rocks to the dry sand above the high-water mark. There I collapsed and fell into a deep, healing Sleep.

When next I woke my Concern was firstly for Water to slake my raging thirst, then for Food and a Fire. I had slept all day and with the setting of the Sun a cold Wind sprang up, chilling me to the bone. A trickle of water issued from the Cliff and ran across the sand. I drank and found it Fresh, but Food or Warmth I went without and passed a Cold and Miserable Night under a bush below the Cliff.

In the morning I knew I must find Food and Shelter or I would Perish. The sea still raged around the sad Wreck of the 'Shearwater', fast on the Rocks some way out. My only escape was up the Cliff, but first I looked around for anything that I might Salvage from among the Wreckage.

There was much Timber. It would have made a fine fire if I'd had the means to light one. My first find of use was a Knife, then an iron Cooking Pot. I found 2 shoes — not a Pair, but I was in no position to be choosy. Then I turned to the Cliff.

In my Weakened State it was a fearful Task to drag myself up from ledge to ledge, clinging to scrubby Bushes as I went, but I reached the Top at last.

Now I could see stretching away to my Right even higher Cliffs, broken and wild in appearance. But to *my Left the Shore fell away and as I stumbled towards this lower Ground I saw a fine sweeping Bay. I resolved to reach it, in the Hope of finding a Settlement of some kind. If only our Vessel had run aground there, how Different my Story might have been.*

I feared to Walk too near the crumbling edge of the cliff top, so plunged in among the Trees and Undergrowth that covers all this Land, marvelling at the strange Ferns that Towered above my head. My Progress was Slow. I was Weak and Bruised but encouraged by the Fact that I seemed to be on a Path of some kind. After some Hours I felt I could go no further and rested on a moss-covered Stone beside a Stream, where I fell into a kind of Stupor.

I was woken by a sudden shove from behind that nearly toppled me into the Water. Standing over me was a tall brown-skinned Man. The rough nudge with his foot was more to see if I were Dead or Alive than to hurt me. Struggling to my feet I saw a Column of People: Men, Women, Children, all Laden with bundles, bags of woven flax, cooking pots and implements. Some led Pigs on ropes. Dogs ran to and fro, sniffing busily. I was not the first White Person they had encountered (I learned later that they had met with both Whalers and Traders) but they were the first New Zealanders I had seen and I fear I stared most Rudely. The Men had swirling Patterns tattooed on their Faces and some on their Limbs also. The Women were tattooed on their Lips and Chins only. I have grown accustomed to them in time, but that First Sight impressed me Mightily and I admit I was Fearful. They offered me no Violence but gave me Food, and when they moved on, took me with them.

Such was my First Encounter with the People I now call my Family. It took me many weeks to Learn that they had gone North to attend the Wedding of one of their Chiefs and had remained there for the Winter. When a Quarrel broke out between the main Tribe and a neighbouring one, they chose to return to the Coast where they could live Peacefully, Fishing and Hunting.

They took me back to their Pa, a kind of Fortified Village, where they settled themselves back into their Homes, Primitive Thatched Dwellings built from some Kind of Native Vegetation.

It took the Natives very little Time to deduce that I had come from a Ship wrecked in the recent Storm. Only a day or two later I saw some of the Men wearing clothes that I recognised. Having found the Bodies of some of my unfortunate Shipmates washed up on the Rocks, they had stripped them of their Garments. At first I was Shocked and Disgusted, but then I thought to myself: Those poor Fellows have no further need for Clothes. Why should they not be put to Good Use?

When I had recovered my Strength, I went with the Men in Canoes to the Place I now call Shipwreck Cove, to see what else we could win back from the Sea. We salvaged timber, nails and sailcloth from the Shore. The Natives are expert swimmers and they dived among the Wreckage, surfacing with all manner of Tools, Cooking Vessels and such like, as well as less useful stuff in the form of Mirrors and cracked plates, all of which caused great excitement when brought back to the Pa.

Finally, another brief but savage Storm broke up still more of the Wreck. Little was left and the Natives lost interest in her and bothered no more with that desolate little Beach.

"I wish he had explained where it was, that beach," said Rona. "We could go and look at it ourselves. Do you know where it might be, Wiri?"

"He called it Shipwreck Cove . . . I reckon that could be Ship Cove."

"What! Right here? But he said it was all bush and trees," Rona objected.

"Well it would've been in those days," explained Wiri. "It was the white settlers who cleared the land and put sheep on it."

"I wish we could get down there."

"There wouldn't be anything to see now. The wreck was nearly two hundred years ago!"

"I know, but sometimes things that have been buried get uncovered again. Like Roman coins being found in someone's garden after nearly two thousand years," said Rona. "Of course, it could be somewhere else altogether. There must be more than one Shipwreck Cove."

Wiri was looking at the diary. "I bet it was this one," he said. "Listen to this."

The Pa was built on a Hill overlooking a wide, far more pleasant Spot where the Shore was less rugged and the Tides less treacherous. There was Good Fishing and I often went out with the Men in their Canoes, or helped gather Shellfish on the Beach.

"See?" Wiri cried.

"See what?" Rona demanded.

"There used to be a pa here, just up behind our farm. It's a protected area. No one is allowed to dig there or anything. It looks out over the bay, and the beach is great for pipis and other shellfish. I bet that's where he lived!"

"I wonder if he wrote anything about the treasure or the ship's bell," said Rona. "Keep reading."

I was of little use when the Men went bird trapping, however. I could not move Silently through the bush as they did and was soon ordered back to the Pa. At such times, left to my Own Devices, I was sometimes overcome with Sadness and Longing for my Home. Then I would take myself off to the lonely Cove and sit gazing out over the Sea, wondering if I would ever see England's green hills again.

But a man cannot Grieve forever and after a while I would be Myself again, Thankful to be Alive and to have found a Home among Good People. Their Life was simple and rough; but so is the Life of a Sailor.

It was on one of my Solitary Expeditions to the Cove that I made a fresh find. It was a warm, still day. At Low Tide, I waded in and swam out to the Sunken Wreck. There I rested, standing on a submerged Spar, water up to my Middle. So Calm was it, that I could peer down through the water at the Keel and the bare Ribs which were all that remained. I could see lumpy shapes scattered all about on the Seabed under a thick layer of Sand.

Filling my lungs with Air I dived in, kicking myself as Deep as I could go. I seized the first Object my fingers touched then shot to the Surface, gasping for Breath as I burst into the Good Air. My Prize proved to be the padded Leather Seat of a Chair. I recognised it as

coming from the Cabin once occupied by Mr Bullivant.
I was about to toss it back when it occurred to me
that if I could fashion 4 legs for it, I would have a
fair kind of Stool on which to Sit.

I peered at the Depths more carefully to see if I
could Identify any other item Worthy of Rescue.

Then I saw it. The Bell.

"The bell!" Rona cried. "Now we might find out
where it is! Quick! Keep reading!"

"I was!" said Wiri indignantly. "Until you interrupted
me!"

The Bell. I had disturbed its Blanket of Sand and
now the brilliant Light of the Sun pierced the water
and lit up its Brass Bowl. No sooner had I seen it
than I wanted it. What use a Bell would be to me or
to any of the Tribe I could not have said, but nonetheless
I was Determined to raise it. I dived again and succeeded
in rolling it over, but I could not Lift it. Even if I
got a Grip on it I realised it would be too Heavy. I
would have to Haul it out somehow.

All other Articles we had retrieved had been handed
over at once to Chief Tanekaha to Keep or Dispose of
as he wished, but this I wanted for Myself. That
being so, I would have to Recover it unaided.

I returned to the Pa where I set about cleaning

and making legs for the Chair seat, but never a Word did I utter about the Bell. I bided my Time until I could slip away unnoticed, taking with me a Strong Rope.

Again and again I Dived, and eventually Succeeded in standing the Bell upright, but still I could not thread the Rope through the Ring on top of it. I had begun my Task at Low Tide. Now the Sea was rushing in and with every Minute that passed the Seabed became further below me. I knew that the next Attempt must be the last for that Day. I dived. I grasped the Ring. I slid one end of the Rope through it; the other end was Secured around my Waist. I took the Rope firmly in my hand and carried it to the Surface. I swam to Shore and began to Haul in the Bell. As soon as it was in Shallow Water I rushed in and lifted it clear of the Waves. It was scratched but nothing that a Good Polishing would not Cure.

I cannot explain the Feelings that moved me as I held that Bell in my arms, but my hands trembled as I traced the Letters engraved around the Lip. SHEARWATER 1795. The Year the Good Ship was Built, None dreaming that she would end her Days at the bottom of some Southern Ocean. Only her Bell remains.

It now stands on the rough shelf I have made against the wall of my small House, my Whare.

This Whare I built myself, a little way from the Pa. It contains a Table and a Stool with a padded Leather Seat, where I sit to Write in this Notebook, and a Sleeping Platform. There is a Box in which I keep my Book and a few spare Clothes, and there is the shelf for the Bell. Rima, my Wife, tells me I should Hang it so that she may Ring it when she wants to Call me Home. I have no Wish to be Summoned every time she fancies she needs my Assistance, so I shall build a Tower for it with a proper Bell Pull and the Shearwater's Bell shall be rung Only on Great Occasions or as a Warning of Danger.

There the reading had to stop for the day. Nan called the children to remind them of the time and Wiri ran home to bring in the cows for milking.

Rona called after him: "Ask your father again about the pa! If it really was just near here we might be able to find where Jonathan Trevarren's house was and where he built the bell tower."

"If he ever built it," replied Wiri. There was still a great deal to find out — and still no mention of the treasure box.

EIGHT

That evening Nan said, "It's Friday tomorrow. I'll be going to town. You can come and have a look in the museum while I do the shopping. They might have pictures or maps of the old pa." Rona had shared with her the latest instalment of Jonathan Trevarren's diary.

Rona was wondering if she could ask Wiri to come too when the phone rang and it was Wiri himself.

"It's market day tomorrow," he said. "Dad's going and Mum and Sissie and the baby and me. I want to check out the museum for old photos. Want to come?"

"That's what Nan suggested," Rona told him. "We're already going in so I could meet you there."

They arranged to meet outside the museum.

Next morning Rona was up early. She put on clean jeans and her tidiest shirt, brushed her hair and tied it back with a red scrunchie.

Nan was looking smart in a skirt and sweater, her shoes polished. She still wore the bone pendant. Rona asked, "Who made it? Is it very old?"

"Goodness knows. It's been handed down for generations. It's only hearsay that it is a shearwater."

"I bet it was made by someone who was on the ship that was wrecked," said Rona.

"Jonathan Trevarren? Mmm, possibly."

"If it was, and it was handed down in your family, that would mean he really was your ever-so-many-greats grandfather, wouldn't it? And mine." Rona was thinking aloud.

"It has always belonged to the Varren family," said Nan slowly, "so this fellow you've discovered would have been *your* ancestor, not mine. I'm only a Varren because I married one, you see."

Rona nodded. It made her feel strange to be uncovering the past of someone who was actually related to her — that's if the name Varren really had been Trevarren originally.

"You won't say anything to anyone, will you Nan?"

"Not until you and Wiri say so," Nan promised.

They waited for Mum's daily phone call from London before setting off for town. Rona used the time to finish her letter to Mum. She could post it in town. When the call came, all Mum could report was "no change". It was hard to do as she said and be patient, but there was nothing else they could do.

The museum was housed in a shabby-looking building, but the interior was polished and tidy. Each room had been restored to the way it would have been a hundred years before. Wiri and Rona wandered around, paying special attention to the photographs on the walls.

The pictures of logging, gum-digging, farming and fishing were interesting, but not very helpful. However, at the rear of the building was a yard, and there they found a model of a Maori meeting house and a long waka, a war canoe. There was a room with carvings and ancient tools of bone and stone and there, too, a row of faded brown photographs. They had been taken in the late nineteenth century and were all of people at work, or in family groups staring solemnly in front of them.

"I guess they didn't believe in smiling for the camera in those days," whispered Wiri.

Suddenly, Rona grabbed his arm. "Look at this one! Read the name underneath." But she read it to him herself. " 'Mr J. T. Varren, surrounded by some of his large family.' It must be Jonathan himself! But they've got the name wrong — it wasn't J. T. Varren, it was J. Trevarren."

The photo, dated 1886, showed an old Pakeha man sitting with his hands firmly clasping a stout knobbled stick between his knees and staring straight ahead. He wore a black suit and hat. A bushy white beard spread over his chest. Around and behind him were gathered a dozen or more Maori men and women, all in dark clothing and with serious expressions on their tattooed faces.

"I wonder how old he was then," said Wiri, doing some rapid calculations in his head. "Eighty or ninety I reckon, if he was in his twenties when he was shipwrecked."

"I didn't know photos had been invented that long ago," said Rona. It gave her a funny feeling to be looking at the face of the man they had been reading about, who had lived all those years ago. Wiri must have been feeling the same because he went very quiet. In silent agreement they returned to the yard and sat on a bench there.

After a minute, Wiri said, "You know, we can't do any more until we've read right to the end of his diary. Let's try to finish it this afternoon and see if we can pick up any clues it gives about the treasure or where he built his house and the bell tower."

The morning was almost over. The two children made their way to the carpark near the saleyards. Nan was already there, talking to Mrs Thompson beside the car. "Ready to go?" she asked Rona. "Nothing you want to buy?" Rona shook her head. "Hop in the car, then," said Nan briskly.

"You too, Wiri," said Mrs Thompson. "Here come your father and Sissie."

"See you later," Wiri promised.

True to his word, Wiri turned up at Shearwater on his bike soon after lunch. "I've got all afternoon," he proclaimed triumphantly. "Mum says she'll get the cows in today. I think it's so you'll have company. We're all really sorry about your father," he added, a little embarrassed.

"Thanks," said Rona. She didn't feel like talking about it. It was good to have something else to take her mind off her worries. She passed the book to Wiri and he began to read aloud:

It is a mark of the Good Favour I was in with Chief Tanekaha that I was allowed to keep the Bell. He could well have made me his Slave, but instead he treated me generously from the Start, Assisting me in Building my small House, and Instructing me also in the Ways of the Bush.

When he saw that his daughter Rima and I had a Liking for each other, he agreed to our Marriage and my Life has become less Lonely. Rima has taught me Much about the Customs and Speech of her People, though laughing greatly at my Mistakes.

As I learned the Maori Tongue I was able to repay Tanekaha a little by answering his Endless Questions about my Life in England and at Sea. He asked me to Teach his eldest Son, Rangi, to Speak English. I could not see what Use it would be to the Boy, but undertook to Teach him as well as I could. My own Parents had set great store by Education and had made sure I could Read and Write. Had they not died of a Fever I would have taken up some Profession ashore, but my Grandfather who reared me had other ideas and sent me to Sea at an Early Age.

But to return to my Story: After raising the Bell I was filled with Eagerness to see what else I could Recover, and the very next day I was back at the Cove at low tide. The Sea was as clear as a Mountain stream. I felt I could reach down and touch the Seabed with my fingers, but it was Deeper than it appeared. I saved my Strength, swimming just below the Surface as I scanned the Bottom for likely Objects. I could make out various shapes of Interest, but nothing that I considered worth the Effort of diving for. As I swam lower, I disturbed a large drab-coloured Fish that had been resting on a Stone, unnoticed by me until it glided away. The 'Stone' glinted Yellow where the Fish had brushed off the sand, and suddenly I realised that I was looking at a small brass-bound Chest that I had Seen but Once before . . . in Abel Parry's hands. I could still hear his Voice: "Share and share alike, Equal for all. We'll be as Rich as Lords —"

Now it could all be Mine, if I could reach it.

"The treasure! At last!" cried Rona. "I wonder what he did with it."

Wiri's mouth was dry with excitement. He gulped down a glass of juice, eager to carry on.

As with the Bell, I was Defeated by the Weight of the Chest, nor could I see any way of getting a Rope around it, Embedded in the Sand as it was. After some Thought I swam ashore and cut myself a long stout Pole. With this in hand I dived again and again,

99

trying to Lever the Chest from its Resting Place. I eventually Succeeded in lifting it a few inches. It now rested on the Seabed, but I was growing Weary and could no longer stay Submerged long enough to get my Arms around it.

I had decided I would have to give up my Efforts for the day and try again when I was Fresh, when I was Alarmed by a long Shadow gliding above my Head. I kicked up and away, fearing some Monstrous Creature of the Deep, but as I reached the Surface I saw it was no Fish but a Man who had joined me.

Tanekaha. Unbeknown to me, he had been Watching for some time, much amused by my Struggles. Seeing me about to give up, he now did easily in a Single Dive what I had failed to do in a Dozen. He lifted the Chest, gave a mighty Push with his Powerful Legs and brought it up. I helped him to rest it on the submerged Spar while he regained his Breath. Then Together we swam ashore, Tanekaha swimming on his Back, supporting the Box.

As soon as he set it down on the Beach, I seized my Knife to Force the Lock, eager to see the Riches I knew lay inside. But Tanekaha put his Hand on my Wrist, restraining me. I looked at him somewhat Impatiently, wondering Why he did regard me so Gravely. He spoke. I had to Hear his words Twice before I

100

made out their Meaning.

"What Evil will you be releasing into the World if you open this Box?" he asked.

How he Knew of the Evil surrounding the Treasure I cannot tell, but Truly, the Disaster that had Befallen the 'Shearwater' and her Crew came from Greed to Possess it. I knew not How to Answer.

"No Evil," I said at last. "It is not What is in the Box, it is the Use to which it is put that makes it an Evil or a Blessing." And with that I gave a Final Twist to the Knife and broke the Lock. Slowly I raised the lid and there was the Gold, the Silver, the little bags of Gemstones, the Rings and Chains, dry and un-damaged.

I gestured towards Tanekaha. "Take what you Want," I told him. "Leave me a Chain or two and do as you wish with the Rest." I wondered if he knew the Value of what lay within his Grasp, but he knew Better than I. He shut the lid angrily then stood up and pushed the Box away with his foot. I was Puzzled by his Behaviour.

"Why are you angry?" I asked, raising the lid to Feast my Eyes once more. "This Treasure could buy all the Tools and Blankets and Seeds you could ever need. New Clothes, better Houses, a bigger Boat —"

"Ae, and Guns and strong Drink," he finished. "When a Man has Pakeha Gold in his pockets he is never

101

at Peace. He Fights to get more or he Spends it as if it Burns his hands to hold it." The Chief picked up a handful of Coins and threw them with Contempt onto the sand. In spite of myself I could not help scrabbling to Collect them all up, even as he Spoke. "I see only Strife and Bloodshed among my People. I see the Land Empty as the Young Men leave it to dwell with the Pakeha. Where the Men go, the Women will Follow. Who will Remain to Care for our Old Ones? Where will be the Children to keep Alive the Customs of our People? Aue!" He ended with a cry of Grief such as did Chill my Spine.

For a long time we knelt in Silence on the sand. I felt he was waiting for me to Respond. I was well aware that he could Kill me and throw the hated Chest back into the Sea and no one would know it had ever Existed, but I did not Believe he would do that.

I could take the Treasure and Leave the tribe, but how Long would I keep it before I was Robbed? How would I account for my Possession of it? I had no mind to be Hanged for a Thief or Mutineer. Until that moment I had had no thought of Leaving, not knowing of any Civilized Settlement within my reach. And what of Rima, my Wife?

At last I said: "I will find a place to Conceal this Box. I will not tell you where it is, Tanekaha, so you will not be Tempted, nor will I tell any other person.

102

We will not Speak of its Existence, so no one will trouble us with Bribes or Threats. It will lie Hidden, but if ever there is a Worthy Need I will bring you as Much but no More than is Necessary. This way the Tribe will Prosper but will not be so Wealthy that the people become Idle and cease to Work for what they Need."

I waited. Finally Tanekaha nodded. "You have spoken well. We will do as you say. I will return now to the Pa and when next I see you it will be as if this Day had never been. We will not Speak of it again." With that he strode away to his Canoe without a single glance behind.

Chief Tanekaha has kept his word and I have concealed the Box where no one will ever Find it without my Help.

"Oh, blast! He doesn't say where he hid it!" cried Wiri.

"What a letdown," Rona grumbled. "I bet he didn't take it far, though, in case anyone saw him with it. It could be still down there on the beach somewhere."

Nan looked in the door. "Don't you two want a break from that book?" Their faces said it all. How could they stop so near the end? "In that case, you'd better stay and eat with us tonight, Wiri. I'll phone your mother, if you like."

"Yes please, Mrs Varren. Thanks."

As Nan's footsteps retreated down the hall, Wiri read on.

NINE

I kept back ten Gold Coins and one small Gold Ring. Then I asked Tanekaha to tell me where the nearest Settlement might be Found. When he understood that I wished only to Visit it and then Return, he willingly lent me a Number of his Men and we set off, carrying all we would need on our Journey.

I will not Record here that Journey, save to say that we walked for 3 Days before coming to a Farm on land cleared by Felling and Burning. There followed more cleared land and the next day we came to the

Town, a poor place compared to olde Plymouth, but bustling with Traders and Seafarers for this Bay of Islands is a Favourite Port of Call for Whalers and Sealers and all manner of Ships needing to Repair the Ravages of the Sea and obtain fresh water and Victuals. It felt uncommon Strange seeing White Faces again, and Folk in European clothes strolling along Boardwalks past Stores and Workshops and Houses with little fenced Gardens and I was in some Confusion at first as to where I should go.

We needed a meal and here I had an Unpleasant Experience. My Native Companions were not welcome in the Eating House we entered. They would serve me but not my Friends. I left in Disgust. We bought Food and ate it under some trees by the River. Before long, my Companions recognised some old Acquaintances and we agreed to separate for a day or 2 until we were ready to return.

It was so long since I had mingled with my own Kind that I hardly knew how to Talk to them. I dared not mention my Ship. I decided to buy the things I needed quickly then find an Inn where I could spend the night. I purchased new Clothing: sturdy, hard-wearing stuff, not forgetting a Dress for Rima and a red Shirt for her Father. The Storekeeper, hearing of my Need, offered me a Bed for the few nights I would be in Town, which Offer I accepted Gratefully.

That night, I enjoyed a huge meal of Roast Meat and English Pudding with as many cups of strong Tea as I could swallow and I slept well in a real Feather Bed with sheets and pillows. I learned, too, that it was the 20th Day of March, 1830.

In the morning I asked my way to a Boat Builder, where I arranged to have a stout Fishing Boat built. When completed, it was to be sailed down the Coast to the Sandy Bay near Tanekaha's Village. I paid half the Price then, the Balance to be handed over on Delivery.

I purchased some blankets, seeds and iron Tools, but there was then nothing more I wanted and I was more than ready to return to the Peace and Calm of my Home, for there was much Drunkenness and Quarrelling in spite of the Mission established there under the Rev. Henry Williams and his Brother.

It was not yet Time to meet my Friends so I strolled about the Town. From one building came the noisy clatter of a Printing Machine and I found there News Sheets for Sale. I bought one, hoping to learn what Events had occurred in the World since I was last in Civilization. I read with Eagerness. New Arrivals were listed, and Departures also, among them the 'Astrolabe' under the Frenchman D'Urville, engaged in Charting this Coast. From olde England came news of the failing health of King George IV. No doubt by now his Brother (Sailor Billy as we called him) is our new King William IV. I read too with Wonder of a steam-driven Engine that runs on Rails at a Speed of 35 Miles an Hour and is called the Rocket. It all seems very far away from my Present Life.

One more purchase I made: this Notebook, Ink and Pens — enough to last me a year — and spent as long choosing them as I did choosing my new Clothes.

It has taken me many days to reach this Point in my Tale. Rima would rather I talked to her, but she is Happy with her new Dress and the little Gold Ring (which she believes I bought in the Town) and does not Bother me.

It will be many Months before I visit the Town again, unless some Need arises that I can satisfy from my little Hoarde of Treasure, which meanwhile lies Undisturbed.

"But where?" muttered Wiri.

"There aren't many pages left," said Rona. "It'll be a bit of a letdown if he never tells us . . . oh no! Maybe it was in the pages that got torn out? Can't you skim over the rest? Just pick out the important bits."

Wiri put the book flat on the table so they could both see it. Now that Jonathan Trevarren had brought his story up to date he only made short entries on days when something of note happened.

This day a sharp Earthquake jolted the Earth causing little Damage but scaring me mightily, this being my First Experience of such an Event. Some of the Cliff fell into Ship Cove, like Cheese sliced from a block. It will now be Most Difficult to gain access to that Beach unless by Sea.

The Fishing Boat I commissioned has been delivered to Sandy Bay. I presented it immediately to Tanekaha who is greatly Pleased. It sails well and will enable the Fishermen to Venture further out and be less at the Mercy of the Weather.

"He's calling them Ship Cove and Sandy Bay now," said Wiri excitedly. "That proves it was here that it all happened!"

This day Rima has told me that she is to have a Child. This has spurred me on to build the Bell Tower for I am determined to ring out my Joy when she is, God Willing, safely Delivered.

"Where did he build it?" wondered Rona. "Turn over and see if he says where."

Wiri turned the page. It was the last.

The Bell Tower is finished. With Tanekaha's help I hung the Bell and it Tolled for the first time since the Wreck of the 'Shearwater'. Its Tone is clear and True, unharmed by its Ordeal. The Tower stands —

"Yes!" cried Rona, punching the air. Wiri grinned and continued.

— The Tower stands above the Cove where the Ship went down. I dismissed the idea of having it close to the House, above my own small Bay. Instead it looks over the Sea, tall and proud, as a Memorial to the poor Souls who lost their Lives, and serves to remind me that as the Sole Survivor I must be Worthy of Life.

"But what about the treasure, Jonno? Tell us where you hid the treasure!" said Rona, impatiently.

I wrote just 2 days ago of my Survival. Today that Life nearly came to a Sudden End. I was casting a net from the rocks at this end of Sandy Bay when a larger Wave than any before swept over the rock and threw me into the Sea. In seconds I was fighting for my Life. I am Strong, but even so I could not Escape the Tide that was carrying me away. I would have been Lost for certain if Tanekaha, my Saviour, had not seen my Plight and swum with a rope to my

Aid. He lashed us together and we were pulled to Safety by those on Shore. This is the second time he has saved my Life, God Bless him.

I have been much Disturbed by my 2nd narrow Escape from Death, and it has occurred to me that if I had Died the Secret of the Treasure would have been Lost with me. I have therefore decided to write Instructions telling where it may be Found, in a Letter which I shall keep in my Box along with this Diary. I have made a Ledge for the Casket, concealed behind . . .

And there the page ended. Rona and Wiri stared in disbelief. They had come so close to finding the answer.

"The letter! Are you absolutely, positively sure there wasn't a letter with the diary?" implored Rona, but Wiri was certain there had been nothing else beneath the floorboards. "Somebody else must have found it before you," she said, glumly.

"Yeah . . . you never know, though," said Wiri. "I certainly haven't ever heard of anyone finding any treasure in these parts. I reckon it'd be worth having a look, anyhow. I wonder where —"

"Ship Cove," said Rona confidently. "It's only a feeling, but we have to start somewhere, and we know he was still going down there because he says — where is it?" She turned back a couple of

111

pages. "Yeah, see here. 'It will now be most difficult to gain access to that beach'. Why would he bother unless he had something special down there?"

It made sense to Wiri, and he had no better suggestion. "Okay, we'll take a look. Can you get away tomorrow?"

"I can get away any time," said Rona a little sadly. "Nan doesn't seem to care what I do."

"Right then. Tomorrow it is," declared Wiri.

Nan had made a chicken and mushroom pie for dinner, followed by bottled peaches from her own trees. "Well," she asked, "did you find out where Jonathan Trevarren hid his treasure?"

"Don't ask," groaned Wiri.

"He wrote a letter, but it's missing," explained Rona. "I bet the same person who tore the pages out of the diary found it."

"We don't know that," said Wiri.

"Why else would they rip up a book?"

"Someone looking for a twist of paper to light a fire, or his pipe?" suggested Nan. "Not everyone could read in those days."

They agreed it could have happened that way.

After dinner Wiri's brother Mark arrived to give Wiri a ride home on the back of the farm bike.

It had been a long day. Rona climbed into bed exhausted and was asleep within seconds.

Dong — dong — dong — dong . . .

Again Rona woke to find the sound of the bell all around her. It filled the room, calling her, and again it seemed to be coming up through the floor.

Wide awake now, she slipped out of bed and into her dressing gown. Flying on silent feet she raced down the passage, determined to trace the source of the eerie sound before it faded. She let herself out the back door and ran along the side of the house to the storage cellar under her bedroom. She lifted the latch and pushed open the heavy door. It was cold inside. The darkness wrapped itself around her like a musty blanket as the door swung shut behind her.

Dong — dong — dong — dong . . . The sound was closer than ever. It had to be coming up from under the ground, but how?

Something warm and silky brushed her ankles. A small, bony head rubbed hard against her feet. She felt its tiny teeth. Rona swallowed a scream as she realised that Mungo must have slipped into the cellar behind her. With a gasp of relief she groped for the door and let herself out.

Mungo's white chest fur gleamed in the light of the full moon. Rona could see the garden almost as clearly as by day. Out here the clanging bell was muffled and distant. It was as if the cellar and her room somehow acted as echo chambers, magnifying the sound. But then she remembered she'd also heard it on the cliff with Wiri. She'd go there now and listen.

As she ran back a light came on in the house. The back door opened, spilling a band of gold across her path and Nan said sharply, "Rona?"

"Er — Nan — I — " she stammered.

"Where are you off to?"

"I was just — I mean, I heard the bell and — "

"And you were going to listen for it on the cliff."

Rona nodded. "Sorry. I didn't mean to wake you."

"You didn't," Nan sighed. "It was the bell. I knew it would sound on a night like this — the moon full, the wind from the west, and the spring tide at its highest. I was lying awake, waiting for it."

"Wiri said it's bad luck to hear the bell."

"They say it's the souls of those lost at sea calling others to join them. I heard it the day your grandfather drowned. Sometimes when it rings I go out on the cliff and think about him." Nan spoke so softly Rona could scarcely catch the words. "But that doesn't mean the bell caused the storm or made the boat capsize," she added firmly, seeing Rona's face. "I suppose I shouldn't have told you that. I probably shouldn't have put you in that room, either. The bell always sounds loudest there . . . but I thought you'd like to be in your mother's old room."

"I do," Rona said quickly. "I just wanted to find the bell."

Nan looked stern. "All the same, I can't have you gallivanting about outside at two o'clock in the morning, especially not up on the cliff!"

"Sorry, Nan. But — "

"No buts. Come on, come inside."

" — but if I do find the bell I'll make sure it doesn't ring again," Rona said, fiercely. She didn't add 'and then Dad won't die' but Nan guessed what she was thinking.

"Come on, back to bed with you," she said. "Bell or no bell, in no time at all your mother will be ringing to tell you the worst is over. Now. How about some hot cocoa? No? All right, off you go then. See you in the morning."

There was no further sound from the bell and after a while Rona drifted off to sleep.

TEN

Saturday morning dawned brilliantly clear and fresh, the sky streaked with crimson. "Too bright," said Nan. "There could be a change in the weather coming."

Rona thought it was just like Nan to see the downside of such a beautiful day. She was sure now that when Mum called she would have good news.

The telephone rang at last and Rona snatched it up. The call was brief. "I don't want to be away from Dad too long," Mum told her.

"Is he worse?" asked Rona, her heart thumping as she heard the strain in her mother's voice. "You've got to tell me the truth, Mum. You promised."

"He —your Dad's had a bit of a setback," Mum admitted. "It's night now and he's asleep. The next twelve hours should tell us one way or another. I —I can't talk about it just now. I'll ring again as soon as we know. But don't worry, I'm sure he'll be all right."

After she'd hung up, Rona looked bleakly at Nan. She felt sick. "I'm going to stay by the phone all day," she said. "I was supposed to see Wiri but I'll ring and tell him I can't go."

"Now what good will that do?" said Nan briskly. How could she be so heartless? thought Rona. "Your mother won't call again for hours. It's night-time over there. You heard what she said —they'll know in the morning. Until then we must carry on as usual. You go and meet Wiri. It's far better to keep busy."

"But what if — "

" 'What ifs' never did anyone any good," declared Nan. "Your father's asleep now. Imagine him resting, getting stronger every minute, ready to wake up on the mend. You won't forget him just because you're not sitting by the telephone worrying."

She was right, of course. Rona collected some food — leftover pie and apples — and rode Wiri's bike down to the farm where she found him waiting for her, bursting with excitement.

"You'll never guess what!" he cried.

"What?"

"Wait till we're on our way. I'll tell you then." To his dismay, she began to cry. "What's the matter? Are you all right? Do you want to sit down for a bit?"

Sitting on the grass, she told him about her father. There was nothing Wiri could do, but telling someone seemed to help. The tears stopped flowing and she said she was ready to go ahead with their picnic, as planned.

"Can I come?" asked Sissie.

"No," Wiri said firmly.

"Why?" she whined. "You never let me go with you anywhere. I want a picnic too."

"Another time," said Rona, feeling sorry for her. "We'll take you on a picnic next time."

"In the orchard?" asked Sissie, cheering up.

"She means in your grandmother's orchard," explained Wiri, "so she can feed the chooks. She's crazy about chooks."

"Okay," promised Rona. "A picnic in Nan's orchard."

"Today," said Sissie.

"No, not today," said Rona.

"Tomorrow?" asked Sissie.

"Maybe," said Rona.

"The day after tomorrow? The day after the day after tomorrow?" Sissie wanted an answer.

"I'll make you a picnic of your own for today," said Maire, who had been listening. "You can eat it in the garden. You two had better get going," she said to her brother. "You can take my bike if you like, Rona. I never use it these days."

"Thanks," said Rona gratefully. "You've got a neat family," she said to Wiri. "Do we need bikes today though?"

"Yep. The only way to Ship Cove is by sea and the dinghy's at Sandy Bay. It'll save hours if we can ride there. Come on, let's go."

The wind on her face cleared away the last traces of Rona's tears as they sped away.

Maire put a sandwich, a piece of cake, a well-scrubbed carrot and a few sultanas in a twist of paper into a bag and popped it into Sissie's little backpack. "There you go, poppet," she said. "Your own little picnic."

Sissie set off. She walked all around the garden

trying to decide on the best place for her picnic. She wandered up to the dam where she ate the cake. In the paddock beside the driveway she ate the sultanas and fed the carrot to Billy, the goat. Behind the woolshed she ate the middle out of the sandwich. Feeling full, she dropped the crust. Then she picked it up again. Mrs Varren's hens would like that. She'd take it to them right now.

She took the shortcut over the paddocks because she didn't like the cattlestop across the gateway at Shearwater. She was scared of falling through the bars. As she skipped towards Mrs Varren's little brown gate, she saw Mungo sitting on a grassy mound a little way along the cliff.

"So come on, Wiri, what's the big secret?" Rona asked for about the fifth time. They had left their bikes outside the store at Sandy Bay and were dragging the Thompson's little aluminium dinghy across the sand.

"Help me push her out and I'll tell you," puffed Wiri, as they reached the water. He was enjoying keeping her waiting.

They scrambled into the boat and Wiri passed Rona a life jacket. "Put this on," he said, pulling his own over his head.

"Are you allowed to do this?" asked Rona.

"I'm not supposed to take the boat out on my own ..." said Wiri, "but I'm not on my own, am I?"

"I don't think that's what they meant," said Rona.

Wiri grinned. "It's okay. I know what I'm doing," he said confidently, taking up the oars. "Well, do you want to know what I found out last night?"

"Nah, not really." Two could play this game, thought Rona. "Oh, okay ... go on then."

"We — our family, the Thompsons — are — wait for it! — we're descended from Chief Tanekaha and Jonathan Trevarren too!" As Rona stared at him, speechless, he explained. "I told them about the diary last night. Mum wanted to know what we were doing at your Nan's house all the time, and Ricky kept on at me about having a girlfriend — "

"As if!" snorted Rona.

" — so to get everyone off my back I told them. Had to. And guess what? Dad went and got this huge great bible — it's massive — and there are all the names of people in our family, when they were born and when they died, written inside the cover. And the first name is Tanekaha!"

Rona's mouth dropped open as she took in the full meaning of what Wiri had just said. "Is — I mean — are Mum's and Nan's names in there?" she asked.

"No, it's only our direct family. Jonathan and Rima had five children. Their names were — " He shut his eyes trying to remember them correctly. " — John, Tui, Awhina, Devon and — um — Alfred. No, Albert. That's right, Albert. But after that it only says who Devon married and his descendants, right down to Dad."

"So why isn't your name Varren, too?"

"'Coz one of my great-great-grandfathers only had girls and their names changed when they got married. The eldest one married a Thompson."

"Wow!"

"Your grandad, Josh, your Nan's husband, must have been the great — I think about five greats — grandson of John or Albert. Probably John, since he was the eldest and you still live in the house that Jonathan built. At least that's what Dad reckons — that Shearwater's built on the site of Jonathan's house. Honestly, I'll never understand my parents. They must have known this all the time and never thought it important enough to tell us. Dad said he didn't know I was interested in stuff like that 'coz none of us kids has ever asked about it." He pulled furiously on the oars.

"But he didn't know what we know about Jonathan Trevarren, did he? Where he came from and how he came to marry Rima?"

"No! That nearly knocked their socks off! You should've seen their faces!" He grinned.

"And we're really cousins, you and me."

"Yep," said Wiri. "I'm a bit more brown and you're a bit more white, but we both come from a Maori chief's daughter and an English sailor."

Rona gave a huge sigh. "I always, always wanted a sister, or even a brother," she said. "Now I have a whole family of cousins and that's even better! It's amazing!"

Basking in her newfound knowledge, she looked at the little waves sparkling all around them as Wiri rowed around the rocky spur to Varren's Bay, at the green hills of the land, dotted with splashes of yellow and purple and rose pink. Sea birds wheeled overhead. Even the cliffs, which could appear so grim and grey, looked beautiful with the sunlight on them.

"I asked Mum why Nan stayed at Shearwater, but I suppose I know the answer now. It's so beautiful. Why would anyone want to leave it, ever?"

If only she could be sure that Dad was going to be all right, she thought, she'd be happier than she'd ever been in her life.

"Mungo! Mungo!" Sissie called.

He ignored her. She'd have to go to him. She offered him the crust but he wasn't interested. All right then, the hens could have it after all. Not the seagulls — Sissie didn't like seagulls much. She looked to see if any were about and that was when she saw the boat, as tiny as a toy, just rounding the rocks from Varren's Bay into Ship Cove.

She recognised Wiri and Rona instantly. Boy, they'd get into trouble when she told Dad. Even Sissie knew that Wiri wasn't supposed to take the boat out without a grown-up or one of the big kids with him.

Sissie jumped up, ready to run home and tell Mum or Dad what she had seen. But if I tell on them, she thought, they won't take me with them next time they have a picnic. Best not to tell anyone.

She looked again at the crust. She was beginning to feel hungry again. Perhaps she'd eat it herself and feed the hens another time.

They had crossed Varren's Bay now and were pulling into Ship Cove. As they reached shallow water, Wiri jumped out.

"Come on," he urged. "Help me drag her up onto the beach."

They hauled the dinghy up under the cliff and looked for something to moor it to.

"Oh well," Wiri shrugged, when they failed to find anything suitable. "I'll just pile a few stones on the rope to hold it down. It'll be safe enough here. We'll be gone before the tide comes up this far."

They looked around the tiny beach.

"I can't imagine climbing up there, can you?" Rona gazed up at the cliff. There was no trace now of any pathway. "How on earth did he do it?"

"There've been a few rockfalls, I guess, since Jonathan's day," said Wiri. The litter of small rocks and a few massive slabs bore out his words. They poked about among them, but found nothing more interesting than driftwood, plastic bottles and other rubbish cast overboard by passing ships and washed ashore.

Suddenly Rona gave a shout. "Wiri! Here!"

He ran to see what had excited her and found her peering into an angle of the cliff. It was in deep shadow and it was not until he was close up that he saw what she was staring at. In the corner, its mouth half blocked by a huge boulder, was the entrance to a cave.

"Man!" gasped Wiri. He stepped inside. Although it widened quickly and stretched away into mysterious shadows, the roof of the cave barely cleared their heads. The air was comfortably cool after the warm sun outside. Wiri felt the sandy floor. It was clean but damp. "The sea must come right in sometimes," he said.

Rona walked around the edges of the cave, running her hands over the walls. She was looking, she admitted to herself, for a hidden ledge or secret niche where a treasure box might have been concealed long ago. She found nothing, but a dark line at shoulder height confirmed Wiri's remark about the sea coming in.

Towards the back of the cave, the roof dipped lower. It was dark, too, but suddenly she realised why. There was no wall to reflect even the faint light that reached this far. Instead there was another opening, leading to another cave.

"I wish we had a torch," she called to Wiri.

"We have," he said. He ran back to the boat and pulled a wooden box from under the seat. He rummaged about among fishing lines and smelly bait tins and came up with a torch.

The batteries were nearly new and shone brightly in the cave. "Okay, let's go," said Wiri.

Bending almost double, they crept through the mouth of the inner cave into darkness.

ELEVEN

As the white torch beam swept across the space before them, the children stared in awe at the vast, swooping cavern surrounding them. The neat, clean outer cave had done nothing to prepare them for this. It was like a cathedral.

"It's — it's like being in a big box of —" Rona had been going to say building blocks, but that hardly described this chaotic scene of tumbled boulders and broken walls.

Wiri understood. "Like someone picked it up and gave it an almighty shake."

They picked their way between the rocks. Here and there, pools of water gleamed briefly as the torch flickered over them, then lapsed into black stillness. Long spears hung down from the ceiling, twisted like melted candle wax into fantastic shapes. As the light touched them, they glistened, wet and white. Other peaks reached up to meet them.

"Stalactites and stalagmites! Wow!" breathed Rona.

"What are they?" asked Wiri.

"Lime in the water that has trickled down through the rock," Rona explained. "It builds up over hundreds of years. You know, like in the Waitomo Caves. I went there once with Mum and Dad when Dad was doing a travel guide thing for the paper."

They went on. Although high-roofed, this cave was not much wider than the first, but it was very long. "I wonder how far back it goes," said Wiri.

"We couldn't get lost, could we?" Rona asked nervously. The weight of all that rock above their heads seemed to press down on her.

Wiri shook his head. "There's only one way out. All we have to do is go back through that archway and we'll be in the first cave."

"Okay, then, we'll see where this takes us," said Rona resolutely.

They ventured further, keeping close together to share the torchlight, until the way forward was blocked by a huge boulder as high as their heads.

"Here, hold this," said Wiri, passing Rona the torch. He gripped the top of the boulder, found a foothold and heaved himself up. He turned around and stood up. "Okay," he said, turning to help Rona, "pass me the torch and I'll give you a ha — *aargh!*" His words ended in a yell of fright as the rubber soles of his trackshoes slipped on the wet rock. He disappeared from sight.

"Wiri?" A groan came from behind the rock. "Wiri? Are you all right?"

There was a pause, then a pained voice said, "Yeah, I'm okay. At least, I'm not really hurt, but — "

"But what?"

"I think I've got a problem. My foot's stuck. It's jammed between a couple of rocks."

"Hang on, I'll come and help."

"Well, be careful. We don't want both of us stuck," Wiri warned her.

Rona laid the torch on the boulder and climbed up beside it. Then, lying on her stomach, she shone the torch down on Wiri. "I see what you mean," she said. He was sitting on a patch of sand with his legs out in front of him. One was bent up but the other was stretched out at an awkward angle, the foot firmly wedged in the rocks. "Look out, I'm coming down."

Rona jumped, landing with a soft thud beside Wiri. She passed him the torch and tried to ease his foot out of the crack. "What goes in, must come out!" she exclaimed, but her efforts soon turned to exasperation when she could not succeed in freeing the foot.

Wiri was now grim-faced with pain. At the last attempt he had gasped to her to leave it, he couldn't stand any more. When she saw how much it was hurting him, it became obvious that she would have to leave him and go for help. Wiri agreed.

"Take the torch," he said. "I'll be all right, but you won't find the way if you can't see."

Much as she hated leaving him alone in the dark, Rona knew it was the only thing to do. "I'll be as quick as I can," she promised.

As she picked her way back to the entrance, Rona wondered if she would be able to manage the dinghy by herself. She had her doubts, but she'd have to try.

She noticed that the sand was wetter than it had been before, and began to hurry. As she reached the outer cave, a small ripple of water ran over her feet.

"Oh no!"

They had been in the cave so long that the tide had come in and was now covering the cave floor. She splashed through the water to the beach. Already it was knee deep out there, and her worst fears were realised when she saw the dinghy bobbing further and further away.

For a moment Rona could only stand and stare helplessly, then she pulled herself together and tried to think what to do next. She looked up at the cliff. Maybe she could climb it? No. She knew she'd never make it.

Waves washed around her. Just how high would they come? She remembered the highwater mark on the cave wall and shivered.

Now a regular stream was flowing through the narrow archway into the big cave. With a sinking feeling, she realised that the floor of the inner cave was lower than the other. And if the water came up to shoulder height out here . . .

She mustn't wait a second longer. She had to get Wiri out, or at least on to his feet so that his head would be above water — she hoped!

Wiri needed no warning. As the sand had become wetter and wetter he had eased himself into an awkward kneeling position. By the time Rona returned, there was a thin layer of water over the entire floor and he was struggling to stand up. With her help he managed to pull himself up, until, with his weight on his free leg, he was leaning against the boulder.

Rona broke the news about the boat. "We're trapped," she admitted. "All we can do is wait until the tide goes down."

"Or until we drown," groaned Wiri. They both wished he hadn't said that. "Sorry," he muttered. "We'll be all right — bet you anything." He did not sound any more convinced than Rona felt.

The water crept up to their knees.

"Climb up on the boulder," Wiri told Rona. "Get as high as you can. No use both of us getting soaked. You'll be all right."

Perched on the rock above the rising water, Rona certainly felt safer, but it was agonising to watch the level slowly creeping up to Wiri's waist. She stayed close to him and chattered on about this and that, trying to keep their minds off their predicament.

"Can you still not move your foot?" she asked eventually, hoping that somehow the water washing around it might have loosened it, but Wiri shook his head. He was still held fast.

"Turn the torch off," he advised. "Save the batteries and make them last as long as we can."

"Give me your hand, then," Rona suggested. Wiri gripped her hand tightly. He did not feel so alone while she was holding on to him and the darkness was not so scary. It was very quiet. The water made no sound as it rose, slowly but surely, around them. There seemed nothing more to say. Suddenly, a faint musical chime shivered through the cave. Rona wasn't even sure she had heard it until she flashed the light on and saw from Wiri's face that he had heard it too.

They listened. It came again, louder this time.

"The Shearwater bell!" Rona exclaimed. As the bell rang yet again, the sound seemed to be all around them. "It's here! The bell's here somewhere! But where? Where is it?"

"It's ringing for me!" Wiri sobbed. Until then he had been totally brave, but the ghostly clamour of the bell echoing around the walls terrified him. "It's not ringing for your father, Rona. It's me that's going to drown!"

Nan was in her studio putting the final touches to the little sea-horse. As she gave it a last buffing and laid it on its bed of cotton wool, she heard the bell singing through the house once more. It had always sounded like singing to her. Then the telephone began to ring and she rushed to answer it. As she listened, relief spread over her face.

"Thank God," she said. "I'm so glad. Rona will

be delighted to hear the news. I'll find her and tell her straight away . . . "

She telephoned the farm, but Mrs Thompson said Rona and Wiri were not back from their picnic yet. "I'll send Ricky to look for them," she offered. "He can nip down to the beach on his bike."

"I'll look on the cliff and around the orchard," said Nan. "I know Rona would want to hear the good news as soon as possible."

Ricky was soon back. "Their bikes are at the store, but they're not at the beach," he reported. "Maire hasn't seen them either."

Mrs Thompson rarely worried about Wiri, knowing how he liked to wander, but this time she felt uneasy. "They've been gone a very long time," she said. "Go and find your dad, Ricky, and ask him to have a look for them."

As Ricky went out the door, Maire came in, and as Mrs Thompson turned around to see who it was, her eye fell on Sissie. Sissie looked sideways at her. Her mother knew that look — it usually meant the little monkey had been up to mischief.

"Come on, Sissie . . . what is it? Do you know something about where they are?"

"Wiri took the boat," Sissie whispered.

"The boat? Where?" Sissie pointed vaguely towards the sea. "Sandy Bay?" The little girl shook her head. "Varren's Bay?" Sissie shook her head again. She did not know that name of the bit of sea where she had seen the boat.

"Next to it," she said.

"Ship Cove!" cried Maire. "They'll have gone to look at the beach where Jonathan Trevarren was wrecked. You know how excited they were about this old diary."

"Of course!" Now they knew where to start looking, everyone sprang into action. Mr Thompson, Mark and Ricky sped down the road in the Land Rover to the village.

"Maire, keep an eye on Bub and Sissie, will you please. I'm going to tell Mrs Varren."

Mrs Thompson took the car and rattled her way to Shearwater.

"If anything's happened to those children, I'll never forgive myself!" Nan cried. "Rona's mother trusted me to look after her."

"You can't watch children every minute of the day," Mrs Thompson pointed out. "All you can do is warn them of the dangers and trust to their common sense. Goodness knows we've told Wiri often enough not to take the dinghy out on his own."

"But I've been so . . . I don't know . . . she must have thought I was very uncaring . . . I just didn't want to make the same mistake with Rona that I made with her mother," Nan tried to explain. "I was too strict with Patricia. It's hard bringing up a child on your own. I wanted to do my best for her and ended up practically smothering her. She couldn't turn around without my being there. I was just so afraid of losing her, too . . . and in the end, that's exactly what I did. She left home at the first opportunity."

"I'm sure Rona knows you care about her, really," the other woman said, reassuringly, but Nan shook her head. The child had looked very lost and lonely at times. She should have shown her how truly fond of her she was.

"I made this for her," she said. She had almost forgotten she was still holding the little bone seahorse.

"She'll soon be back for you to give it to her, you'll see."

Nan smiled gratefully. "Here I am going on about my troubles, and you must be just as worried about Wiri."

"He's very handy with the boat," said Mrs Thompson. "I'm sure they'll be all right. Not that he's getting away with this little escapade scot-free!" she added grimly.

Mr Thompson rang from the village store. The

news was not reassuring. "We've got the dinghy," he reported. "Someone found it drifting and towed it in. The oars are still in it, and the life jackets and their lunch bags, but there's no sign of the kids." He said they were about to set out in a bigger motorboat to scour the beaches. "You stay by the phone. We'll call you as soon as there's any news," he promised.

"No!" Rona yelled at Wiri. "The bell doesn't mean anything! I'm going to find it and stop it. You're *not* going to drown, Wiri. You're not."

She stood up, balancing on her rock, and shone the torch on the walls, moving the beam slowly, searching.

Suddenly she froze. She should have seen it before, she thought, angry with herself for not noticing. The water was not only rising, it was flowing past them to where a long crack split the wall from floor to roof, like a jet black shadow.

"Hey, Wiri! There just might be another way out! Will you be all right if I go and have a look?" she asked.

"Go for it," urged Wiri. He was so cold now that he was almost past caring. All he wanted was to go to sleep. "Get out if you can."

"Not without you," Rona said. "I'm only going to look, but I'll need to take the torch."

"That's all right, I'm not going anywhere." He tried to grin. He had his panic under control now. "Be careful."

Crawling, stepping, balancing, jumping, Rona made her way to the crack in the wall. The water here flowed fast and strong as it forced its way through the narrow opening, but she was able to reach a flat-topped rock and squeeze through onto a ledge. She shone the torch.

She was in yet another cave, cramped and narrow like a shaft. Hanging from the top was a rope, and on the end of the rope . . .

"Wiri! I've found it! The bell!"

A rope attached to the bell's clapper trailed in the rising water. The current rocked it so that even as she watched the clapper struck the brass rim sending out a quivering chime that bounced off the walls and echoed through the caves — and on through many other caves, for all she knew, as yet another opened off this narrow shaft.

As she stood there clinging like a fly to the wall, Rona felt the water swirl around her ankles. She looked down. The flow had stopped. No more was coming in. She gave a gasp of relief as she realised that the tide must have peaked.

"Wiri! We're going to be okay!" she called. "The tide's turning."

There was no answer. The bell chimed softly then hung silent. The water was still and calm.

"Wiri?"

It was too quiet. Something must be wrong. She must get back to him as quickly as she could.

TWELVE

The water was still waist deep, but it had been higher. It was definitely dropping, thought Rona, looking down at Wiri slumped against the rock.

She jumped down beside him. "Wiri! Did you hear what I said? I found the bell!"

The splash she made roused him. "Great," he said, but his voice was weak. "Don't let it ring, Rona, eh."

"No way!" she promised. "We'll be okay, Wiri. The water's going down. Someone'll find us soon."

He managed a grin. "Yeah, sure they will. And we'll tell them to bring out the bell while they're at it, then this won't all have been for nothing."

"They might have to come back for that," Rona began, but Wiri was drifting off again. "Hey! Don't go to sleep, Wiri!"

He opened his eyes. "I can't feel my feet," he mumbled. "They're numb. My legs ache like anything though. I'm so cold."

Rona was worried. She had kept fairly dry until now and was able to keep moving, but Wiri had stood in water up to his chest, scared and in pain. People could die from cold and shock. She had to get help. First, though, she made him take off his wet sweatshirt and T-shirt and put on her dry jacket.

"Thanks," he said, making an effort to help as she pushed his chilled arms into the sleeves. It was hard to think but he knew that without a boat there was no way Rona could get off the beach.

"Have to attract attention," he managed at last.

"How? Shouting's not going to do much good. I could ring the bell, but since no one knows where it is they won't know where to look anyway!"

Wiri did not answer. His eyes were closed. It's

all up to me now to get us out alive, thought Rona. And as quickly as possible.

"Wiri," she said. "Wiri — I'm going back to the beach. I'll wave your red sweatshirt. Someone's bound to go past in a boat or something sooner or later. People will be looking for us by now. I'll have to take the torch. Okay? The batteries are dying anyway. Will you be all right?"

"Yeah, go on." His voice was little more than a whisper.

Rona hated to leave him like that but there was no alternative. Once again she made her way to the outside world, blinking as she emerged into the warm sunshine. The beach was still covered with water. No one was going to see her, waving or otherwise, until she could get further out from the cliff.

She wondered again about the bell. Wiri was afraid of hearing it ring, but if she rang it herself that would be different, not ghostly at all, and if she kept on ringing it, someone might be led to the sound. But what good would that do? She sighed. The bell was nowhere near the outer entrance of the cave. Rona pictured the bell in her mind. There was something . . . as she turned away to go back to Wiri . . . yes! She'd been so worried about her friend that it hadn't registered. When she had turned the beam of light away, the shaft where the bell hung had not been completely dark. That was how she'd seen the rope. Light had been coming in from . . . where? Above?

She draped Wiri's sweatshirt over a rock at the cave entrance and hurried back to him.

"I can't wave yet," she told Wiri. "I'll try when the tide's gone out a bit further. But I'm going to have another look at the bell. The more I think about it, the more sure I am that there was light coming in at the top. What if I climbed the bell rope? Wiri? Wake up!"

Wiri dragged himself up from the darkness he was sinking into. "Couldn't. Too dangerous," he sighed. Why didn't she leave him alone, let him sleep?

"I could try. I climb a rope in gym classes at school." Rona knew it might be dangerous. If she fell it wouldn't be onto a nice soft mat, nor would it help matters if she was hurt too, but she had to do something.

"I'll just have a look. I promise I won't do anything stupid. Don't worry if the bell rings — it'll only be me."

By now, Rona was able to wade through hip-high water to the crack and slip through without climbing onto the ledge. She tugged at the rope

143

attached to the clapper. I'm probably the first person to touch this since Jonathan Trevarren hung it in his tower, she thought. It was a weird kind of feeling.

She stared at the roof. So what's the bell doing here? What happened to the tower? She tried to see up, up through the rock, up through the cliff to the grass that covered it, up to the wind blowing and the sky. She saw in her mind's eye a heap of tumbled timber, fenced off to keep sheep "and nosy people like you, miss" from falling into — what? A well?

What if it wasn't a well at all? What if it was a collapsed bell tower? There would have been no point in repairing the tower if the bell it housed had fallen beyond reach.

Rona released the clapper and it rang against the side of the bell. The noise was louder than she had expected and, startled, she put her hand on the bowl to still it, cutting short the peal.

Her eyes followed the rope as far as they could see it. Now she could see that it was attached to a thick wooden beam that had become wedged across the shaft. That wouldn't be too far to climb. And if there were other beams she might be able to climb right to the top. Would the old rope bear her weight, though?

She swung the clapper hard and the bell rang

again, clanging noisily several times. Then she jumped and caught hold of the rope above the bell, using all her strength to haul herself up until she could wrap her legs around the rope.

Dang — dong — clang — The bell was making an enormous racket in the confined space. She heard Wiri call out to her, but she couldn't make out the words. She yelled back, "It's all right, I'm okay!" in case that was what he'd been asking.

Clang — dong — ding — She inched higher, but now the rope felt different. She knew before it happened that it was about to break. Perhaps the difference was that the strands were snapping one by one. It gave her just enough time to slither down until she was hanging just above the ground. As the last strand broke, she dropped clear of the bell into knee-deep water. The bell landed beside her.

At that moment the last flicker of torchlight expired.

At Shearwater, Mrs Thompson sat by the phone. Nan, unable to sit still, had gone to watch from the cliff top. "I'll just take a look. See if I can see the search boat," she said.

The motorboat was cruising close in to Ship Cove. Nan could see Mr Thompson and the two boys staring hard at the beach, looking for signs of the children.

After a while the boat circled around and headed on towards the next bay. Her heart sank. Obviously they had seen nothing, yet surely it was Ship Cove the children had intended to explore. They wouldn't have gone past it.

And then, as she turned to go back to the house, the bell rang. Not its usual echoing tone, but a timid clang, breaking off suddenly, as if someone had stifled it. She waited but for a long while there was no other sound.

Nan was puzzled. The bell never rang when the tide was going out, only ever when it was a really high tide. She was about to go back and ask Mrs Thompson if she had heard it when the sound came again. Not just one dong this time, but clang after clang, all out of rhythm and somehow flat, as if something was touching the bowl. Then it stopped.

She ran back to the house. Mrs Thompson was at the door, waving. "Did you hear it?" she cried. "The bell! The bell was ringing!"

"I heard it," said Nan. Then she saw the horror on Mrs Thompson's face. "No! It doesn't mean what you're thinking. Anyway, it was different. It never sounds like that usually, and it never rings when the tide's low. Someone must be ringing it!"

"You mean —"

"Yes! The children must have found it!"

"They may have found it," said Mrs Thompson, "but we haven't, and until we do we still don't know where they are."

They stared at each other in desperation. "Well they must be down under the cliff somewhere — or *in* it," declared Nan. "Come on. We'll try and attract the men's attention and get them to look again."

The two women ran to the cliff top. It seemed forever before they saw the boat come into view, powering along at full speed.

"They're heading back," said Mrs Thompson. "Going to do what we should have done at the start — call out the coastguard, I should think. Damn! They'll never see us up here."

"Wave!" ordered Nan. She snatched off her cardigan and waved it wildly. Mrs Thompson burst the buttons on her yellow blouse in her haste to get it off and wave too.

It was Ricky, looking back, who saw them. "Hey, Dad! There's Mum and Mrs Varren. They're waving at us. Maybe the kids have turned up."

"We'll phone from the shop and find out," Mr Thompson said.

"I dunno, Dad, they look pretty frantic," said Mark. "Better go back. Drive in close and let me out, I'll yell up to them from the beach."

Once in shallow water Mark leaped out and ran up the beach.

Crouching low and leaning over the edge of the cliff, Nan shouted down to him. "The children are down there, we're sure of it!"

"We looked right along here, Mrs Varren," Mark shouted back.

"Well look again! Please! We heard the bell. Something was making it ring, and I reckon it must be them.

"The Shearwater bell!" He looked shocked.

"Now don't you get all superstitious as well! It's not a ghost bell. It really rang. It's somewhere down there, and so are the children!" Nan cried.

Ricky had followed his brother ashore. Now he gave a yell of excitement. "Hey! Look! This was on the rocks!"

"That's Wiri's sweatshirt!" cried his mother. "They *are* down there somewhere."

Mr Thompson dropped anchor and charged ashore to join his sons. "Where did you find it, Ricky?"

"Over here . . ."

They disappeared out of sight from above. All the women could do was wait. No one reappeared. The empty boat rocked, seagulls called, and still they waited.

Rona left the greyish gloom of the shaft and groped her way back to Wiri. She wanted to take the bell with her so he could at least feel it, but although she could lift it, it was too heavy and awkward to carry while feeling her way safely. The clamour of the bell had shocked Wiri into wakefulness. Now his voice guided her towards him. "You should have stayed there, where there was a bit of light," he said.

"Nah. If we're going to be stuck here, at least we'll be company for each other. Tell you what, though — I'm starving! I keep thinking about our lunch floating out in the boat somewhere," said Rona, her stomach rumbling. "Anyway — I'm sure they'll find us soon."

"Do you think you could find your way to the beach and try waving now?" Wiri asked a few minutes later.

"I could try," she said doubtfully. "But if I can't find my way out, you'll have to talk me back here, okay?"

She moved slowly, testing each foot before she trusted her weight to it. She tried to remember the way she had gone earlier, but it was so very black, and everything seemed different. After a long time, she still had not reached the wall.

"Wiri?" she called in a small voice.

"I'm still here," he called.

Rona stood still. He sounded much nearer than he should have been. She hadn't been moving away from him, she'd been going in a circle around him!

"This is useless! I'm just going round in circles," she cried. "Can you whistle or something and I'll keep going away from the sound."

"Okay," said Wiri, struggling to stay alert.

Rona crept forward. She bumped into rocks and grazed her knees. She was very cold, too, and dreadfully hungry.

"What?" she called, thinking she heard Wiri call her name.

"I didn't say anything. I'm just about talked out."

"Rona! Wiri!" The voice came again.

Rona burst into tears. "We're here!" she yelled. "We're here! Wiri, they've found us! Somebody's found us!"

It was the next day before Rona saw Wiri again. The rescue party had spirited her away to her grandmother's and Mark had stayed with Wiri while his Dad took Rona home and collected the tools he needed to chip away the rock around Wiri's foot. He brought warm food and drink and blankets for Wiri, and spotlights too, for by this time it was almost dark. The tide was on its way in again before they were through and the rescuers carried the boy out through deep water.

Wiri was kept in hospital overnight, suffering from mild hypothermia. He could have been much worse if it had not been for the constant temperature in the cave and the lack of wind chill. He was allowed home the next morning on condition he stayed in bed. His ankle was badly swollen and still strapped up when Rona came to see him.

"It's not broken," he said. "Just sore. Did your Nan tell you off?"

"No," said Rona.

It had been an astonishing time since the rescue. First Nan had hugged her as if she had really meant it. Then she had told her about her dad. He had made such a dramatic improvement that Rona had been allowed to talk to him herself when next her mother phoned. He and Mum were going to come and stay for a while with Nan once he was fit enough to make the long journey back to New Zealand.

"Actually, Nan gave me this," Rona said, showing Wiri the little carved sea-horse. It hung around her neck on a leather thong. Nan had hugged her again when she gave it to her.

Wiri was admiring the pendant when they heard

voices outside. "Are you ready for a surprise?" Rona asked.

The door opened and in filed all Wiri's family and Nan too. Last of all came Mr Thompson, and Wiri gasped as he saw what his father was carrying. "The bell!"

It was polished and gleaming like gold. Mr Thompson put it on the bed. Wiri traced the letters around the rim: S-H-E-A-R-W-A-T-E-R 1-7-9-5.

"Nan's going to have the tower rebuilt and hang the bell again," Rona said.

"But not over a fault in the rock this time," added her grandmother. "Jonathan Trevarren couldn't have known it, but he built his tower right above a weakness in the limestone. It was probably an earthquake that opened it up — the tower collapsed and the bell disappeared."

"Until we found it," said Rona.

Wiri had to ask. "Did you look for the treasure?"

"We looked all right," said his father. "There's nothing there, I'm afraid."

"For all we know it may have all been spent," said Nan. "Jonathan Trevarren — or Varren as we know him — built the house he called Shearwater, and he built this house for his son Devon. The youngest son died, but he was probably just as generous to his daughters."

"And it was a Varren who built the school and the church in the village," added Mrs Thompson. "There couldn't have been much left."

"I wonder if it was hidden in the bell tower?" murmured Wiri. "If it fell when the tower collapsed, it could still be down there."

"Oh no you don't," warned his mother. "No more caving for you, my lad!"

"I bet he's right though, even if this is all there is," said Rona, pulling something out of her pocket. She held out her hand. On it lay two black coins. "When the rope broke, I landed on my hands and knees and as I pushed myself up again I felt these. I stuffed them in my pocket and forgot all about them until now."

She handed one to Wiri and one to Nan. "They are gold, don't you think?"

"Certainly looks like it," said Nan.

"Wow!" said Wiri.

Rona gave a sigh of contentment. Dad was getting well, Nan loved her, and she had discovered a whole family of new cousins. She and Wiri could share the last of the treasure, even if it was only one coin each, and the Shearwater bell was going to have a place of honour in Nan's garden.

"I brought the diary, too," she told Wiri. "I guessed you'd like to show it to your family now."

"I'll get it!" cried Sissie. Before anyone could stop her she had darted away and moments later was back with it.

"Look out!" yelled Wiri, as Sissie tripped over her own feet. The book flew into the air. Maire caught Sissie and Rona snatched up the book just centimetres from the floor.

"And this," she said, "is going into a special glass case. Isn't that right, Mr Thompson?"

"Certainly is. This is as big a treasure as the bell. Forget the gold. Between the two of you, you've found enough treasure for any family."